# CLAIMING HIS BEAUTY

## FERAL BREED MOTORCYCLE CLUB
## BOOK FOUR

# ELLIS LEIGH

Kinship Press

Claiming His Beauty
Copyright ©2015 by Ellis Leigh
All rights reserved
ISBN: 978-0-986371-6-4

Kinship Press
P.O. Box 221
Prospect heights, IL 60070

For the readers...

# ONE



"YO, ZIPPO. THAT MOVIE you like so much is on." I flopped back against the couch cushions, popcorn bowl in one hand and beer bottle in the other. It was almost eight, and the good movies were about to start on cable. Just knowing that probably meant I needed to get out of the house more, but riding the couch watching movies had somehow become my typical Saturday night. At least it had ever since I moved back to Detroit from the western side of the state and gained a couple of witches for roommates.

*Two witches and a wolf shifter walk into a bar…*

Flipping through the DVR, scowling at the amount of reality shows saved, I blew out a breath. Living with other people in my den was wearing on my nerves. I was itching to head west, to the quiet, empty little cabin I usually called home. At least there, the only way I had to deal with people on a regular basis was electronically. The town was shit-poor, which meant most of the clientele at my auto shop had to trailer in their classic car or drive them from hours away if they needed service. I built custom rides off specs emailed to me, sold most of my vehicles over the internet, and dealt with actual people as little as possible. But hell, apparently I was worth it because my email had been blowing up ever since I shut Yard Shark Customs down to hang in the dirty D. And while the break from work was nice, it was about time to go home. Alone.

"Sorry, Cujo. Not tonight," Scarlett said as she raced into the room. Glancing up, I nearly dropped my beer, my eyes opening wide. The woman was definitely not dressed for a Saturday on the couch. Her red hair was all curly and kind of up, yet dangling a bit, she had fancy jewelry on, and there was some fabric covering her that probably would have passed for a dress if it'd been about six inches longer.

"Where the hell do you think you're going?" I growled. The rough tone was unintentional but not something I could hold back. Scarlett had become someone I honestly cared for, practically family in my head. Unfortunately for her, that meant I paid attention to the little things. The way her skin flushed pink as she dug through her bag, how the smell of her excitement wafted around her, and the fact that there were no panty lines showing through the thin-as-fuck fabric of that... not dress. She was definitely about to do things a brother would frown upon. So I frowned, placing my beer on the side table, crossing my arms over my chest, and raising the only eyebrow I could to make my point clear.

Scarlett turned to face me in a slow spin. Something about the way she moved, all measured and exact, made my hackles rise and my balls tighten up. That turn was something dark and unnatural, kind of like the *Exorcist* kid's head before the pea soup started spewing.

She gave me a look that almost made me want to submit to her, to cock my head and expose my neck, my inner wolf spirit not used to such a display of power. Even the ends of her hair glowed—a sign of her favored fire element flowing through her—telling me exactly how pissed off she was. If there was one thing I'd learned in the past two months living with these girls, it was that you didn't fuck with a fire witch if you didn't want to get burned. Literally.

Her sister Amber walked in at that moment, glancing from Scarlett to me as she made her way to the couch. "Am I right on time, or did I just miss the fireworks?"

"Shut it, Miss Cleo," Scarlett said, earning a bird flip from her sister.

I snorted a laugh. Amber was an air witch who happened to be skilled in the power of precognition. Fire-starter and future-teller…my life had become a carnival attraction.

Scarlett took two steps toward me, her eyes burning with anger. "Are you trying to be some kind of authority figure all of a sudden? Because, trust me, I don't need a daddy in my life, Beast."

Amber settled next to me and grabbed a handful of popcorn, raising her eyebrows as I glared at her. When she smiled and winked, I rolled my eyes and went back to staring down Scarlett. These Weaver women had bigger balls than most of the men in the Feral Breed Motorcycle Club dens I'd been in.

"Don't get your nonexistent panties in a twist," I said, lips curling back in a snarl when Scarlett made a noise oddly reminiscent of a growl. The wolf side of me snapped his jaws, stalking forward and refusing to back down to the woman even with all the power she held. "I just want to know where you're going and why you didn't tell me you had plans."

"I didn't realize you were the plan police." Scarlett pivoted on her heel, grabbing her coat off the rack. "But since you're so concerned, I have a date."

A record scratch sounded in my head. A date? Neither girl had gone on a date since we'd moved to Detroit in December. Hell, Scarlett rarely left the townhouse, refusing to even step foot in the den house a few blocks over and avoiding all my Feral Breed brothers. I wasn't sure what the protocol was in regards to her dating. Was I obligated to act in a familial role since Phoenix, a man I saw as a little brother, was mated to her sister? Or was it better to just toss her a strip of condoms and tell her to wrap it before she rode it?

I rubbed a hand over my face, tugging at the ends of my beard as I stared at the irritated woman. "Scar, it's not like—"

A horn honked outside, making Scarlett jump. Biting her lip and taking a deep breath, she wrapped a scarf around her neck and pulled her gloves out of her pocket, giving me a weak smile over her shoulder as she headed for the door. "You two behave now. Don't have too much fun without me."

And with that, she was gone, leaving behind nothing but the scent of her perfume. I stared at the spot where she'd disappeared from, an anxious feeling making my wolf instincts flare. Wrong—the night felt altogether wrong all of a sudden.

Instead of talking about her sister's unusual escape, Amber handed me the bowl of popcorn. "Looks like it's just you and me."

I shrugged, no longer completely comfortable. Amber had lived with me for as long as Scarlett. I liked both of them, but I'd never spent a lot of time with the elder air witch. Shit, before the girls had fallen into my life, I hadn't spent much time with people at all. Not since my pack days. But Phoenix had mated to the youngest of the triplet witches while on a mission to the western side of the state. I'd offered up my home to the two sisters who refused to be separated from Phoenix's mate to make it easier on him. The poor guy was tight as could be with money and only had a studio apartment—there was no way he could fit all three of the girls plus himself in that shoebox. So it was me and two witches in my three-story den, which was only a few blocks from Phoenix's place. One woman a human flamethrower and the other some kind of psychic. A psychic who was staring at me as if she could see inside my head... which I guess she kind of could.

"*Pitch Perfect* or *The Breakfast Club*?" I asked, desperate to fill the silence.

Amber shrugged, pulling a string from her pocket and tying a single knot in the middle. "Got anything harder?"

"Harder as in…" Raising my eyebrow, I leaned back in my seat. The knot tying had me on edge, my wolf spirit wary. Phoenix's mate Zuri had taught me a bit about the magick the girls practiced, from the elemental powers they controlled to the stuff they'd learned as children. Spells cast with colors, candles, and salt. There was also plenty of magick to be made with knots tied in thread. Like the one Amber was playing with.

"I like to watch stuff blow up." She leaned across me, taking my beer from the table and bringing the glass to her lips. Two swigs later, she pulled it away with a smile, handing it back to me. Staring into her eyes, I suddenly had the oddest urge to down my beer. A feeling of being overly thirsty when I'd been fine just seconds before. Unable to resist, I tipped the bottle back, draining it in seconds.

A grin spread across Amber's face. "While I enjoy a cold beer as much as the next person, I wouldn't mind a night with Jack or Johnnie, depending on what you have handy. I'll just go grab a bottle."

"Yeah, sure," I said, unsure why my lips were tingling. "Harder is good."


THREE HOURS AND A *Transformers* movie later, I was drunk. Not really drunk, just comfortably so. Almost numb. Or maybe that was just my nose. But my cock was definitely not numb. Nope, it was nestled against a warm, willing witch who'd straddled my lap at some point in the last…who the hell knew? And when the fuck had I gotten drunk enough to allow Amber to do what she was doing?

Too much. Something about the moment was too…too… too… Damn, she felt good. I ran my hands over her waist, grabbing her hips with both hands and pulling her tighter against my erection. Rubbing on her. This was such a bad idea, but it was mating season. That had to be why I couldn't stop from biting her shoulder and pressing my hips into hers. Mating season. If I could just catch my breath, I might be able to…oh God, yeah…right there. Fuck, I literally couldn't stop myself.

With a sigh, Amber untangled herself from my arms and sat up, pushing my shoulders against the couch. My head lolled back, my inner wolf howling. Something wasn't quite… Amber ran her fingers over the ink on my forearms, following the patterns. They were supposed to mean something, those lines and swirls, supposed to be important. But I couldn't remember just then. Not with the feel of her fingers tickling my skin.

As she dropped her head forward, Amber's long, dark hair spilled down her shoulders and over her chest. Teasing her breasts. My eyes followed the movement, zeroing in on the hard nipples pressing through the thin fabric of her shirt. My hands wanted to follow, but my arms were too heavy. I couldn't lift them from where they gripped her hips.

My wolf spirit howled louder and longer, creating a cacophony of sound that slowed my senses, made me forget something big. Something important.

Amber dragged her hand up my arm and over my shoulder, all slow and careful. The howl in my head turned to a ferocious growl but not soon enough. I froze half a second too late, too out of control to realize Amber's destination until I felt her fingers against the rough and rigid skin left behind after a battle that'd almost killed me. A patch of skin that hadn't been touched by anyone other than me in decades.

"Show me how you got your scars."

Light and sound exploded behind my eyes, my memories screaming as they played out. Shadows dancing behind flames, a cabin burning bright against a desert sky. And the screams.

Cracks and pops from the fire that devoured my home were mere whispers in comparison to the voices. Names…prayers… wails of pain. All because of one stupid decision. Because we'd trusted—

I growled and jerked my head back and forth, expelling the past that tore my heart from the walls of my chest, my head clearing as centuries-old anger and pain raged through my blood.

"What the fuck is going on?" I hissed, trying to push the girl off my lap, my arms finally waking up.

Amber's face fell, but she didn't apologize. And she sure as hell didn't let go of me. My head cleared a little more, smoke and desert air replaced with the metallic scent of ozone. Amber stared over my shoulder, her wide eyes unfocused. Her Magic Eight Ball look, as Scarlett called it. Leaving the present behind to look into the future. I fought back a shiver—the concept of seeing things that hadn't yet happened creeped me out. It was intrusive, and the so-called gift would seem to me to bring a sense of arrogance to the gifted one. Because she may have seen the events coming, but that didn't mean she could act on what she saw. What her magick allowed her to know. What… oh hell, what had she done?

Putting one hand on my chest, that damned knotted thread hanging between her fingers, Amber stared hard into my eyes. "What's your real name?"

A picture of my mother slammed into my consciousness, her lilting voice washing over me. That smile, that laugh…I couldn't believe I'd forgotten. I hadn't purposely thought about her in decades, but there she was, whispering to me. "Bas-tea-ahn," she'd said, pronouncing the name I'd shared with her father in three syllables instead of two. "Bas-tea-ahn, my prince. Go to sleep before the faeries come."

I almost smiled, the whimsical childhood stories she'd loved to tell coming back to me, but my father's voice was next. And it wrecked me.

*"Pray, Bastian. Pray to never find your mate. Pray to keep your soul to yourself so it is never ripped in two like mine."*

I gasped, my hands curling into fists, my wolf spirit forcing its way past the haze inside my mind. Breaking through the magick being used against me.

Picking Amber up off my lap and tossing her on the couch beside me, I growled, "Undo it."

Her eyes went wide, but she didn't speak.

I snarled and grabbed her wrist, the piece of thread still dangling from her fingers. "Whatever you've done, un-fucking-do it. Now."

Amber stared at me, challenging, but my wolf spirit enraged was not something to fuck with. I hadn't earned my road name of Beast by backing down or talking things out. I gripped her wrist, not feeling the least bit guilty for the grunt of pain she released as I twisted.

"Undo what you've done, or I'll break it."

She stared a moment longer, not moving, but then I twisted harder. With a squeal, she dropped the thread and snapped the fingers on her free hand. The thread ignited, burning from both ends toward the middle. I released her as the ashes fell to the floor, the final weight of her magick falling away.

"What the fuck, Amber?"

"She needs you, but you're not..." She paused, eyes bouncing left to right, seeing something I couldn't. "Your mate is in trouble."

Every breath I'd ever taken blew out of me at once.

I'd heard the expression "my heart nearly stopped." It always made me want to laugh at the idiots who said it. As if they actually felt their heart *almost* stop in their chests. Like that was a possibility...to *almost* feel something. And then Amber said what she did, and my heart did a weird kind of pause in my chest.

Fuck me running; you really could feel your heart almost stop.

I'd spent over two hundred years mateless, certain in the fact that I'd never be blessed to find my fated match. Not after the mistakes that took my parents' lives. Not after the scars and the prayers and the deaths. And yet, deep down, I'd held on to a tiny string of hope. Like a sinner in those first moments of confession, just before they bowed their head to admit their wrongs, I'd hoped for some kind of higher power to clear me of my past transgressions. To forgive me, and to provide me with that love bond. My brother had found his mate this past year, and I'd watched Phoenix find his the first time his eyes met Zuri's. Watching had only made the need within me glow brighter, and tucking away that hope had grown more difficult.

Fighting back a desire that had been buried under fire and scars and deaths, I sat up, leaning forward with my elbows on my knees. "What the fuck are you talking about?"

She looked me in the eye, wearing an expression too close to guilt for my liking. "I've been having these flashes for a while. Tiny bits of visions, but nothing strong enough for me to figure out the context, you know?"

"No. Not at all."

Amber sighed and brought her hands up, her fingers almost dancing in the air. "Imagine you find a picture, a single snapshot of a moment. Maybe there are ten people in it, all laughing and smiling. You have no idea who they are, how they're connected, where they are, what they're doing, but you can see that one moment in time, and you make guesses off of it. That's what my visions are sometimes like."

"So you're more of a Polaroid than a Magic Eight Ball?"

She scowled. "Look, I've been seeing this woman for weeks. Same one, same place, same picture. It's driving me crazy because I can't put her into context. But I have a feeling she's tied to you."

"Tied to me?"

"Yes, tied. Literally. I think she's your red thread." Her eyes were wide, almost manic as she leaned closer. "I have this urge to show her to you, as if it's something I have to do. As if you really *need* to see her."

"So you did some kind of voodoo and climbed into my lap?" I asked, standing up and stepping away from the couch. Away from her.

"I had to feel it."

I raised my eyebrow.

Amber huffed. "Not that, you...*man*. I needed to be physically close to you to feel your end of the thread connecting you to your mate. You're too much like Scarlett; both of you have it buried deep under the rubble of past mistakes. I didn't see another way."

I rubbed a hand over my face, my neck burning with the anger I was trying to hold in check. "So you felt it was okay to put me under a spell, crawl into my lap, and do what you wanted? To use your magick against me?"

"No." She shook her head, breaking eye contact. "I just needed physical contact for a few minutes, and I knew you wouldn't let me be that close without a little intervention."

I sighed, fighting back the urge to punch the couch. Or a witch. "Amber, this was really fucked up. You can't just—"

"I know, and I'm sorry. It was wrong to trick you, but"— she looked up, eyes practically glowing—"your mate needs you. I couldn't wait any longer."

A chill screamed down my spine. "I don't have a mate."

"Of course you do." She looked into my eyes, drilling deep, as if trying to see into my soul. The air stirred around us, imparting secrets over our skin as it passed, secrets I'd buried in a desert long ago. My mouth went dry, my chest tightening as the clock ticked the passing time.

"*Bas-tea-ahn.*"

I closed my eyes at the whisper of a memory, suddenly missing my lost family members in a way I never had before. Prayers like church bells resounded in my head. Words of contrition and apology, of thanks and of need. Pray for us sinners, indeed.

Filled with an emotion too unfamiliar to name, I let go of a chain I'd been holding on to for many years. And for the very first time, I voiced my biggest fear. "I don't think I deserve a mate."

Amber cocked her head as I opened my eyes, her face filled with a confidence I didn't feel, edging on relief. "Everyone deserves love, Beast. That's all a mating bond is. It's a primal connection brought about by destiny, forged of love, and held together with fate and faith. Isn't that what your father taught you?"

Her words were a punch to the gut, a physical pain carried on a language that suddenly seemed foreign. Because they sang of the truth, of the lessons my parents had given me as a pup. A truth conveniently forgotten.

Minutes later, I stood in the same place, staring at nothing, letting my thoughts trickle to where they wanted to go. Amber had long since left, heading upstairs with nothing more than a smile in my direction. But I couldn't turn off my mind, my memories doing battle with my dreams.

*"Pray you never find your mate."*

Sighing, I finally forced myself to move, mentally exhausted and ready to end this crazy night.

Once I'd cleaned up and locked the doors downstairs, I climbed the stairs to my room on the third floor. Plain and bare, it could have been a room in a hotel. I'd always preferred my home sparse, no secrets to give up should someone be stupid and nosy enough to intrude. But tonight, the lack of anything personal cried of something missing. Something lost.

Giving up all attempts at figuring out why I was suddenly

uncomfortable in my own space, I fell onto my bed and pulled a pillow over my head. But as I slept, pictures of past events barraged my dreams. Fire and blood, screams and tears. I woke up more than once, sweating, fisting the sheets to keep from shifting to my wolf form out of panic. By three in the morning, when I woke for the fourth time with my heart racing in my chest, I gave up the guise of sleep. Whatever energy Amber manipulated to get me to open my mind to her must have fucked with my brain. I was trapped in the hell of memories I'd sooner have forgotten.

Frustrated and tired, I trudged downstairs, making a pit stop at the liquor cabinet for a bottle filled with whiskey. No glass, no ice, and no chasers, I tossed back a few mouthfuls. The amber liquid would hopefully be the answer to my insomnia.

I yawned as I entered the living room, shuffling my way across the wood floor. Lying back on the couch where my life had turned down a strange path a few hours earlier, I put my head against the pillow and closed my eyes. Not that I expected to sleep… But then, the entire night had been a bit of a course in the unexpected.

Sleep did find me, and when I began to dream, it was no longer the past I saw. Or if it was, it wasn't a past I remembered. I dreamt of a restaurant, one I didn't recognize. But Amber had been wrong—what I saw wasn't a frozen image or a photo; it was more like a video clip. A repeated scene lasting a handful of seconds. On the first run-through, I noticed the restaurant itself. The tables were mostly empty, the sky outside the windows dark. The old pleather seats were well past their days of being in decent condition, but the place looked clean and the food looked good.

But those things weren't what held my attention as the scene repeated over and over.

It was a woman. Short with light brown hair, she had a tired smile on her lips as she carried a tray across the floor. There was something about the look in her eyes that called to me, something about her that drew me in. And when she glanced up as if I'd spoken and her eyes met mine, my body tensed and my cock swelled, growing so hard, the pain was enough to rip me from my dream.

I woke with a snarl, my fingers tipped with sharp claws as my body began the process of shifting to my wolf form. I gritted my teeth and held on to my human form, though barely. My wolf was enraged, my mind filled with explosions of color and sound as the two sides of my spirit fought for control. The wolf edged ahead, fur sprouting along my body as my teeth lengthened. But then my human side recovered, fighting back my shift, clinging to the only thread we had left to hold on to. Escape.

Finally, after being trapped between forms for more minutes than I cared to think about, I relaxed my sweat-covered body and fell to the floor. Fuck me, that was a close one. I was still lying in a state of not-quite—part-wolf part-man. But at least the human side of me was in control of my mind, my wolf spirit having retreated to the darkest corners once more. When the fur and claws finally receded and I was fully human again, I raced up the stairs, growling the entire way, my chest burning with a rage I couldn't tamp down.

Storming through my room and into my closet, I threw a bunch of clothes in my black duffel bag and opened my safe. Inside was my secret stash of The Draught, the drug my den president Rebel had concocted. It had a sedentary effect on shifters, calming their wolf instincts and allowing them to behave more human. I normally avoided the stuff, but I was about to lose control of my wolf and I knew it. I downed a small vial and tossed the rest of them in my bag. I had enough to last me for a couple of weeks if I needed it. And I probably would. The wolf inside me had to be muzzled for a while.

Grabbing my bags, I ran back down the stairs, ignoring

the sound of Amber and Scarlett calling my name. This was Amber's fault… If I saw her while this out of sorts, I might do something I'd regret later. And Scarlett was involved by proxy. So instead of stopping, I ran to my truck and peeled out of my driveway. Let the witches stay in the house—they didn't need me there to babysit them. Besides, witches and wolves didn't mix well. That reminder was just kicked into my head.

I was almost to the state line when my phone rang on the seat beside me. I thought about tossing the damned thing out the window but knew that would only make things worse. If I went off the grid completely, Rebel would have every Feral Breed member from across the country looking for me. And right then, I really needed to be left the fuck alone. Which meant dealing with at least one person.

I answered the phone on the fourth ring. "What's up, Phoenix?"

"Why don't you tell me? I just got off the phone with Amber."

I growled, my hand gripping the steering wheel hard as just her name sent another flare-up of anger through me. "Nothing's up. I'm just feeling a little claustrophobic and tired of hanging out with witches. Figured a week or so away would do me good."

Phoenix grunted. "You're sure that's it?"

"Yeah," I replied. "I'm good, just really fucking stressed. I need a few days on the road, man."

"Okay." Phoenix murmured something I couldn't hear, probably talking to his mate and the third Weaver triplet, Zuri. "Beast?"

"Yeah?"

"Call me if you need me, okay? I'll come…we all will. No matter what."

I didn't answer, guilt turning my stomach sour. Phoenix and I had been through a lot together. As his wolf giver, I was the one who was supposed to look out for him, and yet this time, our positions seemed reversed. Still, we'd known each other for too long to bullshit one another. There was no need for added words or promises we already knew the other would hold up. He was my blood; he'd die for me just as much as I'd do the same for him.

Finally, Phoenix sighed. "I'll tell Rebel you'll be out of pocket for a few days."

"Thanks," I said, my voice tight.

I tossed the phone on the passenger seat and reached inside my bag for another dose of The Draught. Fuck me, my wolf was clawing at my mind. I had to go…to run…to escape from everything before I exploded. Battling to keep my fingers from turning into claws once again, I pressed my foot harder on the gas. The roar of the engine revving gave me a little thrill, so I did it again until I was flying down the highway at over a hundred miles an hour, my scarred face pulling into the closest approximation of a grin it had as the dotted white line turned solid. I needed to get away. Needed to get my head back on straight before I dealt with this whole Amber thing.

Because I'd flat-out lied to Phoenix.

My leaving wasn't about stress; it was about what Amber showed me. Not so much her deception, which was an entirely different issue, but more the results. Her little spell gave me a glimpse of my mate all right. Short, light brown hair pulled up in a ponytail, with a tired smile as she walked across that damned restaurant. I'd known she was meant to be mine from the second I saw her, even though it'd only been in my mind. But I couldn't have her. Of that much, I was certain. The woman in my vision was beautiful and sexy, with warmth in her eyes that told me she'd have a good soul, a good heart.

She was also quite obviously pregnant.

# TWO

*Calla*

"ORDER UP."

I finished pouring the coffee at table two and headed for the service window. My smile stretched my face, feeling too big and bright—almost plastic—but I kept it on, ignoring the looks and whispers. I'd been showing for months. You'd think they'd have gotten used to me already.

Mannie smiled a real smile when he saw me standing at the pass-through. "Table five, please."

"Thanks." I grabbed the plates and weaved my way across the floor, turning and twisting between the chairs as best I could. It was getting harder to fit lately, something I was sure Mannie noticed. So far, he hadn't commented on how slow and awkward I'd become, but I knew it was coming. I just hoped he could see how hard I was working for him every day. He'd given me a job when I was desperate, when no one in this town would even give me an interview. Waitressing at the Highway Line Diner was a crap job, but it was the only crap job I could get, and I was grateful for it.

"Here you go, hon." I set down the plates and smiled at the burly oil workers about to dig in. "Anything else I can get you?"

The men shook their heads and grabbed their forks, too worried about filling their bellies to give me more than a passing glance. Not that I minded—invisibility was something I strove for as the months went on. Something my pregnant belly made impossible.

I made my way over to Mrs. Littman, mother of the mayor and one of the regulars at the diner. And a total snake in the grass. Straightening my shoulders and plastering on my brightest smile, I prepared for battle.

"Anything else I can get you, ma'am?"

She looked me over, her eyes hard and her lips curled into a frown. "You do know having sexual relations before marriage is a sin, don't you? Sex between a husband and his wife is the only form of relations of which our good Lord approves."

I gritted my teeth and grabbed her empty pie plate. "Yes, ma'am. As I've told you many times already, I've read that same passage. If there's nothing else, I'll just go get your check."

Stomach sour, I was halfway across the restaurant when I heard her mutter "slut" under her breath. The same way she did every night at the end of her meal. My grip on the pie plate turned painful, and I wished for just one second to be anywhere but at work. It took everything I had not to spin around and give her a piece of my mind, but as always, my reality gave me a kick in the gut. Or rather my baby did. With no one to rely on but myself, and my little angel due in a matter of weeks, there was no way I could lose this job. I needed the money more than I needed to march over there and set the old blue-hair straight. At least that's what I kept repeating in my head.

The rest of the night went about as well as I could have hoped. While my baby wiggled and hiccuped in my belly, I smiled, charmed, and walked about a thousand miles across the diner floor. I did my best to keep my head up and not let the more conservative locals see how their harsh words stung. Oh sure, they smiled and asked me how I was doing, how the baby was doing. The women tended to ask all the regular questions about pregnancy: When are you due? Do you know what you're having? How are you feeling?

But as soon as I walked away, the judgment began. The darted glances, disapproving looks, and the whispers. Sticks and stones could do some damage, but words hurt worse than anything.

They talked among themselves about how horrible it was that I was an unwed mother. How I likely didn't know who the father was. How they knew I was screwing around with those animals who worked in the oil fields. That one, the comment about the oil workers being animals, always made me roll my eyes. If these people knew the animals living in this town—the real ones, not the men in the fields who tended to get into a little trouble with the law now and again—they'd run away screaming.

Something I probably should have done when I found out I was sleeping with one.

By the time I flipped the sign on the door to closed, my legs were burning, my ankles were swollen, and my back was positively throbbing. Being on my feet all day was not what I'd planned when I moved to this little town, but plans had a way of falling through. And mine had fallen hard. What I wouldn't give to be back in Minneapolis, whining about my boring desk job every day. But if I'd never come here, I never would have been blessed with the little angel who seemed to have a fascination with kicking my ribs. With a smile and a rub to my side, I focused back on the job at hand. No sense in rolling over old stones or living in what-ifs.

I was wiping down the tables when Mannie came out from the back with his coat on.

"Gotta go, Calla. There's a storm coming in, and I don't want to get stuck in it. Are you almost done here?"

I nodded. "Sure thing, boss. I'm just going to finish the

four-tops, and I'll be heading out as well."

He paused, indecision on his face. Mannie and his wife lived almost an hour away, while I could practically see my building from the front door of the restaurant. He often left me alone to close up, not that he ever seemed comfortable doing it.

"I can wait for you—"

"Don't you dare." I went back to wiping the table. "Get home before the storm hits. I'll be done in a couple of minutes and on my way."

He sighed. "Okay, if you're sure."

I waved him off as I scrubbed, not looking his way. Once the tables were wiped, the floor was sparkling clean, and all the lights were turned out, I left out the back. The cold stung when I stepped outside, and I shivered as I let the door close behind me. The lock latched automatically, which was why Mannie asked all the employees to use it at night. He couldn't give us all keys to the front, even though it'd be safer to park under the lights and where people could see us from the neighboring gas station. Nope, we had to park around the back of the building, where there was no overhead lighting and no way for anyone to see should we need help.

And damn it, if the growling I heard coming from the edge of the woods was any indication, I could really use some help.

He stepped out of the blackness like a wraith, like the very image of a nightmare. Tall and dark, he walked with a smoothness and a confidence I'd once found appealing. But not anymore. I'd learned the hard way what was under that fancy coat and those fake manners. I knew the animal within. Intimately.

"My beautiful Calla." He stopped right in front of me, practically trapping me against the side of my car. "You're looking lovely tonight, my sweet. How are you feeling?"

I held my breath as his hands went to my swollen stomach, but I didn't jerk away from his touch. I refused to show him a single sign of weakness. Still, I was suddenly thankful for the extra layers of down and nylon my coat afforded between my skin and his.

"I'm fine, Aaric," I said, keeping my voice as calm as I could. "What're you doing here?"

His eyes flashed in the shadows surrounding us, glowing slightly in the dark. That inhuman light was probably the creepiest thing about him, one of a long line of creepy things I'd learned over the year we were together.

"Watch your mouth, little one, or I might stick something in there to keep you busy." He moved closer, a wolfish smirk on his face as I recoiled. "I've missed being inside you. I'd prefer your cunt, but I'll take your mouth if that's your preference."

I couldn't help the way my face screwed up in a scowl. He waited as I held my tongue, probably looking for any reason to dole out some kind of punishment or hoping that I'd take him up on his offer. But the time I'd spent with the man had taught me well. I bit my tongue and choked back any response I had. Better to stay silent than play his mind games.

After a tense minute, he smiled a sickeningly sweet fake smile that made the hair on the back of my neck rise. "Perhaps another time."

I glared, still not saying anything. He was out in the cold for a reason, and the longer I kept my mouth shut, the faster he'd get to the point.

"Are you taking care of yourself?" His hand once again moved to stroke my belly, this time the tips of his fingers curved into claws. I shivered as I stared at that hand—part human, part animal. One hundred percent scary. I wanted it off my body and away from my baby. Or, unfortunately, our baby.

"Of course." I took a step back, forcing his hand to drop off my stomach. His eye twitched, his only response at the little show of my rebellion. He still thought he held dominion over me, but he was wrong. He just didn't know how wrong yet.

"You can always move onto pack land," he said, stepping closer, pushing me into the side of my car with his body. "I'll keep you fed and happy until she arrives." His hand creeped over my belly possessively, finally sliding up under my coat. Feeling the warmth of his skin sent chills up my spine and made my heart pound as I fought back a bout of nausea.

"No." I shook my head, trying to force myself to calm down when silver spots appeared in my field of vision. "I'm fine on my own."

"Suit yourself," he said with a shrug.

I held my breath, doing whatever I could to hold still as the spots grew. Sparkles I'd called them when Aaric's nurse had come to check on me. She'd warned me the spots were a sign of high blood pressure and to relax whenever I noticed them. Too bad it was hard to relax when trapped by a predator.

One claw-tipped finger scraped across my belly, cutting my shirt and pressing against my overly stretched skin. I doubted he'd risk his precious baby by hurting me, but I was near enough to my due date for the baby to live outside of my womb. It was entirely possible he'd begun to see me as dispensable.

Finally, he pulled his hand away and sighed. "Keep my pup safe for me, Calla. Once this is over, I'll give you everything you need. Money, a new car, a place to go. Whatever you want, you'll have. You can leave here, start a new life for yourself."

My chest tightened and my cheeks burned as rage flowed through me. "Not without my baby."

"You need to realize that's not going to happen. You have two choices, my sweet. Give me the baby and stay here on pack land to help me raise her, or give me the baby and leave. There's no other option for you…if you want to live, that is." He smirked, his eyes glowing brighter. "I'll see you tomorrow, lover. Or maybe I'll send the pack. My boys wanted me to tell you it's about time to try to run again. They've been missing you, I think."

He spun and disappeared into the dark as quickly as he'd arrived, leaving me clutching my chest and trying to catch my breath. My hands shook as I dug for my keys and opened the door, my legs nearly giving out when I swung my body inside. Aaric had a way of showing up at just the right time, right when I was beginning to believe I could escape from him and this town. From the horror of his pack of wolves. But trying to escape had already cost me so much.

Tears burned my eyes as I started the car, and my shoulders slumped. I was beginning to think I'd die trying to escape. I'd tried numerous times and failed, his pack of inhuman madmen hunting me down before I'd even made it out of the county. The first time had been painful, Aaric punishing me with his claws for trying to leave. The last time had nearly killed my soul. I closed my eyes as the memories came back, silently praying as I waited for them to pass.

*Hail Mary, full of grace. The Lord is with thee. Blessed art though amongst women…*

Calming, shoving that horrible night to the very back of my mind once more, I contemplated how to get away from Aaric. The man was evil through and through, and I wanted nothing to do with him or the animals who followed him. Too bad he was so sure my daughter was going to be one of them. Too bad for me, at least. Because as afraid as I was of the wolf shifters who lived in this town, there was no way I was going anywhere without my baby.

Desperate and sinking into a despair unlike any I'd experienced since the night I'd been attacked by Aaric's pack, I looked up to the sky through the windshield. The stars shone bright against the velvet black, something pretty in the middle of the ugly world in which I'd found myself trapped. Giving into the desire within my heart, I swallowed and reached for the cross I always wore around my neck, the one my grandmother had given me upon my confirmation. One of the few things I had left from that life.

Face cold but heart open, I wrapped my hand around my talisman, and I prayed. *Please Lord, keep us safe. Please help me find the way to save my family. I need help.*

# THREE



I PULLED INTO THE gas station on fumes, both figuratively and literally. I probably should have stopped in one of the bigger towns I'd passed along the way to wherever the hell I was, but I'd been being chased by the demons of my own mind and unwilling to even slow down. Still, fifteen hours behind the wheel without a break had left me fucking spent. I needed a good meal and a bed, though not necessarily in that order.

As I filled the tank in the truck, I let my head fall forward, exhaustion heavy on my shoulders. It had been a long-ass week. Something—some kind of force or energy—had been chasing me from the time I left Detroit six days prior. I'd tried to fight it, but that just made things worse. Every time I paused, the pull inside of me told me to keep going, keep moving. And every time I slept, the vision of my mate, my very pregnant mate dancing in the flames that'd taken my parents, assaulted me. I was slowly being driven mad, the past and the impossible future coming together to torment me in ways I never thought possible. So I'd stopped fighting the urge, driving in circles and straight lines for days. I'd been through twelve states and down an untold number of highways before ending up in this

Godforsaken town. This place would never have been my first choice for somewhere to stop—a one-light town at the western edge of fucking North Dakota in February was nowhere near where I wanted to be—but it was as far as I could go on this stretch.

I finished pumping the gas and crawled back in my truck, too weary to go any farther. Let the demons come back; I couldn't push myself another mile. Surrendering to my need for sleep, I drove into the lot of the only motel on the main drag. The place was a dump—too old and too far off the tourist track to get much in the way of guests. Perfect for someone craving privacy.

Trudging through the cold, I headed for the lobby door, bones aching and face burning from the wind. My wolf senses were buried so deep under the effect of The Draught that I barely noticed the guy behind the desk as I stepped inside.

"What can I get ya?"

I grunted, uncomfortable with how little I'd sensed. Six days of heavy Draught use had really messed with my wolf. Eyelids heavy, mind slow, I reached back for my wallet and tossed a card on the counter. I needed to sleep. A lot. "One room. Two nights."

The clerk nodded, looking a little nervous. Not that seeing humans in fear was anything new. Whether it was my scars, my ink, my beard, or just the overall package of a wolf in sheep's clothing, I'd been giving humans an adrenaline rush for decades. Usually I'd ease back a bit on my shifter side, but without my wolf senses to guide me, I couldn't tell what made him want to shit himself. Fuck it…the guy was just going to have to deal.

Once the clerk handed me my key and pointed me on my way, I lumbered up the stairs and toward the door leading to my salvation, otherwise known as a bed. The room was dark, dank, and smelled of sex and stale cigarettes, but it would do. I'd slept in worse.

After tossing my bag on the bed, I headed for the bathroom. Clean but outdated, the room boasted a leaky faucet and a showerhead I'd have to duck to stand under. Wonderful. Turning on the taps, I thanked the fates for at least letting my ass land in a place with a working hot water tank.

As I stood under the hot spray, my thoughts turned once more to the image of my mate. The way her blond curls fell to her shoulders. How her uniform top showcased her plump breasts. And the tiredness on her face. That was what haunted me. There was a sadness about her, and the fact that she looked as exhausted as I felt made my wolf want to surge past the drugs keeping him at bay. My mate shouldn't be so tired. She should be cherished and cared for, not exhausted and pale, especially while carrying a child. I hated knowing that whoever the father of the baby was, he wasn't taking care of her as he should have. Wasn't protecting her. Was failing her as I'd failed my mother years before.

But those were all things I shouldn't try to fix.

I wasn't any kind of saint, but I could respect the bond of family. I'd tried time and again to zero in on her hand, to see if there was a ring denoting a sacred bond. Unfortunately, the hand in question was in shadow, and it was too hard to determine if she was married or not. Either way, she was carrying another man's offspring. I would never tear apart a family, which meant I needed to stay away from her. I couldn't risk the pull of a mating bond on a woman who'd already decided her path was with another.

Clean, dry, and just about dead on my feet, I fell onto the bed completely naked, almost immediately falling asleep. But not for long. Once again, images of my mate haunted my dreams. I awoke time after time, either filled with rage that I couldn't have her, terrified that I'd have to watch her burn in the flames of my past, or horny as fuck. Hell, I was about ready to rut against the mattress all because those pink lips of hers looked so fucking soft. But I resisted. This was another man's wife, or at least his chosen partner. I had to respect the claim of another, no matter how much I wanted to keep her to myself.

Five hours later, after being woken up by yet another dream resulting in a raging hard-on, I crawled out of bed. There was a diner down by the gas station that had signs boasting they were open until ten. It was only eight-thirty, so I pulled on my jeans, threw on a long-sleeved thermal shirt, and slid into my Feral Breed leather coat. If I couldn't have sleep or sex, at least I could have food.

The same clerk was behind the desk when I strode into the lobby.

"That diner down the road any good?" I asked, trying to keep the growl out of my voice. The guy's eyes widened for a moment before he nodded.

"Yeah, Mannie makes good food. Try the meatloaf; it should be on special today."

I gave him a wave of thanks as I headed toward the door. When I stepped outside, the bitterness of the cold made me catch my breath. It also woke my ass up. The temperature must have dropped a good fifteen degrees since I'd arrived. The wind screamed across the flat lands, swirling snow to the point that I couldn't tell if the frozen white wall was coming from the already fallen piles or if it was fresh. My wolf would have loved to run through the woods in this kind of weather, but he was so drugged, I doubted I'd even be able to shift. Which was a bit of a sobering realization.

I could see the restaurant sign from the motel parking lot, but there was no way my ass was walking. Jumping into my truck, I revved the engine and gave her a few minutes to warm up as I dug inside my glove compartment. Pulling out a glass vial, I sat back and stared at the dark liquid inside. The Draught. I'd need to find more soon, which meant reaching out to other shifters. Being a member of the Feral Breed, the lawmen of the shifter community, could make that a little tricky seeing as I didn't know the packs out this way. I didn't want to make them think I was chasing a man-eater, but I also didn't want anything getting back to my den about my whereabouts. I'd turned my phone off the morning after I'd driven away from Detroit, and I wasn't ready to deal with the calls I was sure were coming in from my brother and denmates.

"Fuck it." With a sigh, I bit the top off the vial and downed the dose of The Draught. A few more days—that was all I wanted before I began to deal with the reality of losing the one thing I'd never even hoped to have. A few days and I could ease off the drug and let my wolf wake up. Maybe by then I'd figure out a way to control his need to find our mate.

Throwing the truck in gear, I backed out of my spot and headed down the road, quickly reaching my destination. But as soon as I opened the door, my shoulders stiffened. The scent of wolf shifters hung in the air like a warning, strong enough to push past the dulling effect of The Draught. Other wolves didn't usually bother me, but with my senses so blanketed by the drug, the last thing I needed was a confrontation. Requesting a meeting and showing respect while shopping for more Draught was one thing, having an angry pack hunting me down for invading their territory was something completely different. I'd definitely be leaving after my two nights were up.

Stepping inside the diner, the scent of wolf was replaced by the warm smell of homemade food. Burgers, eggs, bacon, and something almost flowery…all of it making my mouth water. I settled at the counter, ignoring the old woman at one of the tables who couldn't stop staring. As my arms were covered, it had to be either the motorcycle club jacket or the scars. Normally, I would have ignored the old crab, but I was still tired and running on anger. So instead of taking the high road and turning my back to her, I made sure to angle myself so she could get a good long look at me. Slipping out of my coat, I pulled up my sleeves to showcase my ink as I flexed the muscles in my forearms. Let her get an eyeful of that as well. Pretty sure she'd leave before I even ordered—

Lust. It hit me hard, a tidal wave of need pulling me under and stealing my breath. I whipped my gaze around the room, trying to discern what about this place had me suddenly needing to adjust myself. Cheap tables, pleather seats past their prime, good food on tables… And that was when the panic blew up inside of me, followed closely by a sense of dread tinged with excitement.

I knew this place. Had been dreaming of it for days. Had seen it numerous times, though without saturation of color. The picture I'd watched repeatedly had appeared almost black and white, but reality was not a mental picture. This place was bright but still familiar, and that meant one thing. She was here…the woman with the warm smile and tired eyes.

My mate.

I'd followed the pull inside of me and ended up halfway across the country, sitting at the counter in the restaurant where she worked.

Of all the fucking luck.

# FOUR

*Calla*

THE WIND WHIPPED PAST as I hurried into the diner, the cold settling deep in my bones even on the short walk across the back parking lot. If I somehow got out of this place, I was going somewhere warm, where I didn't have to don fifteen pounds of clothes just to go outside. The back door slammed closed behind me, the welcoming warmth of the restaurant making my eyes tear up. The cold would be bitter when I left after my shift, and I crossed my fingers that my old junker car would start. And that I wouldn't run into any more trouble in the back lot.

Once I'd hung up my coat and dropped all my winter gear in the closet that served the employees, I hurried out on the floor. I avoided eye contact with the regulars as I made my way to the front, already dog-tired. I'd spent the morning scrubbing every inch of my apartment. "Nesting," the experts called it, but that was way too soft a word to describe the kind of cleaning I'd done. My eyes were red from the bleach fumes, my back was sore from bending and leaning into every corner, and my hands were positively ragged. Next time, I'd have to remember to wear gloves.

"Let's go, Calla," Mannie hollered. "These eggs aren't going to deliver themselves."

I tied my apron and rushed toward the service window with a smile pasted on my face and my head held high. Today was going to be a long day, and I needed to start it off right.

Six hours later, I leaned against the back wall of the building, huddled against the cold. My hands were tucked underneath my heavy down jacket, rubbing my swollen stomach. The cramps I'd experienced for the past few days had gotten worse, and I was in more pain than I'd expected. More than likely, the pain was from a lack of water and too much time on my feet. I'd tried keeping a glass of ice water behind the counter, but Mannie didn't like his waitstaff eating or drinking in front of customers. So I stood outside on my break with a big glass of water resting on a ledge by my side. I rubbed my belly, and I prayed. Just a few more weeks, and my little one would arrive.

Weeks. That was all I had left to plan. If I didn't get out of town before the baby was born, Aaric would take her from me. I'd be trapped in his pack because there was no way I could leave her behind. Just the thought made me want to hit my knees and sob. Aaric had once been so kind and charming, but he'd shown his true personality after I'd gotten pregnant. Violent, abusive, and not at all someone I wanted around my child, he'd managed to trap me in a situation that suited his needs and destroyed my own. I had to run, but after what happened the last time, I was afraid. Too afraid to act on my own.

Heart heavy with the weight of my growing hopelessness, I grabbed my water and headed back inside. Just a few more hours and I'd be going back to the shabby little apartment I'd called home for the past year. My prayers from the night Aaric had cornered me in the back lot echoed in my head, a petition of sorts. Or perhaps a simple wish to find a way out of here. But I was beginning to think that wish had fallen on deaf ears.

The diner was relatively empty, just a couple of oil workers sipping coffee, old Mrs. Littman at her usual table, and a man I'd never seen before who was sliding into a seat at the counter. He was big like the men who worked the fields, with skin a bit more golden than mine had ever been, even with a tan. Tall and muscular, he had a mop of dark hair peeking out from beneath his black knit skullcap. His jeans and black combat boots didn't speak to working outdoors, though, and the black leather jacket clinging to his wide shoulders was practically a beacon for some of the bikers who traveled through town in the summer. But it was winter and the snow had been falling for months; no biker would ride through at this time of year.

By the time I made it around the counter, my mystery guest had taken off the jacket and pulled up the long sleeves of his thermal shirt. Color exploded as the gray fabric slid away, revealing patterns and pictures that ensnared my gaze.

Loud, bright art covered nearly every inch of his forearms, a beautiful message that probably should have screamed a warning. And it did...sort of. His shoulders, broad and stiff, were a testament to his strength. The way he sat with one foot on the ground as if ready to jump into battle was a sign screaming *stay back*. The curve of his neck as he turned his head—giving me a peek of the dark, rough beard covering the lower half of his face—an animalistic move that should have made me run.

And yet, there was something about him, about the man hiding beneath all the trappings. He didn't make me nervous like some of the truckers and oil workers did. In fact, I felt drawn to him. Intrigued perhaps by the ink and beard, so far removed from the straitlaced professional men I'd spent most of my time with in the past. So I walked to him with no fear, my eyes searching out his.

"Can I get you something to drink?" I asked as I stepped in front of him. Bright blue eyes the color of a cloudless sky on a summer day met mine. Warm eyes...kind. He stared at me for a beat, those eyes traveling over my face as if inspecting me.

Wanting to know me.

I did the same, concern making my heart heavy as I noticed the bags under his eyes and the sallow quality of his skin. He looked almost sickly, as if he hadn't slept or eaten well in a long time. I followed the line of his dark brow, and that was when I noticed the scars. They ran from just above his eyebrow all the way down and under the beard; thick, heavy pink scars that told the story of brutality and aggression. The scars reminded me of my own; the ones Aaric added to my body when I'd run the first time. The ones his packmates had added to the last time.

When his eyes met mine once more, they were filled with an expression of warmth and concern. I wanted to live in that look, cling to him and be the person who earned his interest. But then he pursed his lips, and his expression changed. An intentional blankness appearing that stung far more than it should have.

"Coffee."

His gruff response stabbed into me, making me wince. His eyes widened, that veil of noninterest slipping.

"Sorry," he said. "Coffee, please. Black." His eyes met mine again, his lips pulling up in an uneven smile.

"Sure thing." Ducking my head to hide my burning cheeks, I turned and rushed to the drink station. The man had me blushing like a schoolgirl and all he'd done was ask for coffee. Stretching over the edge of the counter, my belly totally in the way, I grabbed the pot from the machine and brought it back. Mystery man sat still as a stone, watching me, his eyes intense.

"Here you go." I filled his cup, doing my best to keep my hands from shaking. Lord, he smelled good. Like leather and something dark that was uniquely man. It was a scent that made me feel comfortable, warm, and exceptionally feminine.

"Thank you," he murmured as I finished pouring. His fingers wrapped around the old ceramic mug in a gentle grip, and yet there was so much strength there. In the way his muscles moved, the way they made the colors covering him dance. I'd have bet money his hands were callused and rough, the hands of a man used to hard work.

"You're welcome." I smiled again, pushing down the thoughts of his hands on mine…on me. Pregnancy hormones really could make you feel crazy. "Would you like to order, or are you just here for the coffee?"

He hummed as he brought his cup to his lips, the sound making my mind drop right into the gutter. It'd been so long since I'd even had the energy to think about sex. Aaric hadn't touched me since I'd told him I was pregnant, and for that, I was grateful. But not even my battery-operated boyfriend had seen the light of day in months, my body too tired and uncomfortable to feel in any way sexy. And yet, this man, this armored study of masculinity, made me feel completely aroused by doing nothing more than drinking coffee.

"What's good here?" His deep voice pulled me from my inappropriate thoughts. He'd grabbed a menu out of the holder and had it lying on the counter in front of him, his long fingers skimming the plastic pages.

"The stuffed cabbage is always good, and the meatloaf that's on special today is one of the local favorites." I raised my eyebrows as his gaze met mine. "Or if you want something lighter, the salads are on the back."

His lips turned up in a smirk. "Do I look like a salad guy?"

I shook my head, my face growing warmer. "No, definitely not."

"What's your favorite?" he asked, his tone serious as if he actually wanted to know. "When you're really hungry and want a good, hearty meal, what do you get?"

"Pot roast." My answer came out as a whisper, soft but deliberate. "My favorite comfort food is pot roast, and Mannie's is the best around."

He sat back in his chair, that investigative expression back in his eyes as he looked me over. "Pot roast it is."

I gave him a nod before hurrying to the service window to place his order. I only had the two men with their coffee left in the diner, having not noticed Mrs. Littman leave. Forcing myself to get back to work, I brushed past the mystery man at the counter and went to refill the cups across the room. Space… space was good. Being close to him made my mind fuzzy, made me want to do things I knew better than to try.

When the stranger's food came up, I delivered it with a smile before heading to wipe down the tables. It was almost closing time, and I didn't want to get stuck at the diner alone again just in case Aaric came back. Aaric, who looked like a yuppie businessman but had a violent streak a mile wide. Contrasting him with the man at the counter had my smile sliding into a frown. Mystery man was exactly the opposite—or so it seemed. Rough on the outside, with a charming smile and a calming presence that made me feel safe around him. But I'd been wrong before when it came to men. Wrong to the point of ending up in a dangerous situation I saw no escape from.

After the pot roast, my mystery man ordered a piece of blueberry pie and another cup of coffee. By that point, the rest of the customers had left and Mannie was closing up the kitchen. I finished wiping the tables and swept the floor, doing my best to ignore the man at the counter. Not that he was easy to ignore. My eyes continually found him, usually meeting his as he stared right back at me. The tension he made me feel grew with every glance, every stolen look, until I could hardly breathe from the pressure.

When ten o'clock passed, Mannie came out from the back. "Is there anything else I can get you before we close?"

The man shook his head. "No, but thank you. And thanks to your waitress for recommending the pot roast. That was the best meal I've had in weeks."

"Ah, that's good to hear," Mannie said with a smile. "I like to know my food hits the mark, and Calla here is one of the best waitresses we've ever had." Mannie glanced at me, his grin turning to a look of concern. "Norma wants me home right away. Do you need anything before I go?"

"No. I'm fine."

He glanced at the man sitting at the counter, who was just finishing his fifth cup of coffee, then back at me. Questioning. I waved off his concern. If there was one thing I was relatively sure of, it was the fact that my tattooed stranger wasn't going to hurt me.

Once Mannie had left, I turned the open sign to closed and locked the front door. Back behind the counter, I picked up the empty coffee cup and saucer and dropped them on the pass-through ledge to be washed in the morning. When I turned around, he was watching me again. His eyes unfocused, his smile small and slightly sad.

"Calla," he said. "It fits you."

"Really?" I shrugged. "My grandmother told me it meant castle."

"Kind of. More fortress, something strong and worth protecting."

His words set my heart racing. The man was such a contradiction. All hard edges and rough exterior with a soft smile and an air of sweetness. I liked it; liked him. More than I probably should have. This was the absolute worst time in my life to develop a crush though, as the baby in my belly reminded me with a sudden, singular kick.

Knowing this was the end of our little flirtation—if that's what anyone would call it—I quietly said, "I can let you out the front if you're ready."

The unfocused look disappeared, his eyes zeroing in on me with quick precision. "What about you?"

"What about me?"

"Who walks you to your car?"

"It's just me…and my little girl here." I laughed, rubbing a hand over the curve of my belly.

His eyes dropped to my stomach, his stare intense. "Does she have a name yet?"

I shook my head. "No. I figure I'll know what to name her when I see her face. At least I hope."

"Sounds like the perfect plan." He smiled, his eyes filled with concern when they met mine again. "Why don't you finish up and I'll escort you out? It's too dark for you to be safe out there alone."

"I don't even know your name. How do I know it's safe to be alone with you in the dark?" I asked, the words slipping out without thought. The double meaning making my cheeks burn again.

"I'm Bastian." His smile fell, his face growing more serious. "I'm no danger to you, Calla. I swear it."

His words rang so true, his voice so honest, that I couldn't not believe him. I nodded before walking down the hallway to grab my jacket, not wanting to make him wait any longer than he had to. Once I was ready to brave the frigid night air, I turned off all but the security lights, leaving us in shadows that ratcheted my attraction to him up even higher. I was definitely not safe with him in the dark, not if I wanted to keep from making a fool of myself.

Internally reprimanding myself for letting my thoughts roam so uncontrollably, I pointed toward the back door. "I'm out this way."

Bastian stood with a grace that was almost unnatural, his body uncurling from the tall stool with ease. I stared as he pulled his sleeves down and put his jacket on, those wide shoulders once again making the leather pull tight. Tall, big, and obviously strong, the man was a living, breathing billboard for masculinity.

He approached with a slight smile on his face, his arm held out in my direction. "After you."

We walked out together, the cold slapping me in the face as soon as we stepped outside and switching my thoughts from "he's so dreamy" to "I'm going to freeze to death" in a moment. I curled into my jacket while the wind howled past, desperate for the warmth that seemed to be just out of my reach. When my teeth began to chatter, Bastian placed an arm around my shoulders and pulled me into his side.

"I'm practically a furnace. Stay warm until you get out of this wind."

I melted into his hold, my heart nearly breaking knowing I'd be saying goodbye soon. Once we reached my car, he dropped his arm, making my stomach bottom out with an intense sense of loss.

"Thank you, Bastian," I whispered, trying to hide my sudden sadness. "For…everything."

He stared down at me, his eyes hidden by the shadows falling across his face. I had an irresistible urge to touch him, to kiss him, to hold on to him. To learn everything about him. So I did.

I ran a finger along the ink I knew to be on the back of his hand, following the swirl up to his wrist. When my skin found smooth leather, I paused. "Who are you hiding under there?"

Bastian didn't say anything, but he didn't pull away, either. Emboldened, I lifted my hand higher, bringing my fingers to the scarred flesh of his face. Barely brushing his jawline.

He must not have been prepared for my touch because he jumped back, a rumbling coming from deep within him. A noise I was familiar with. One that made me gasp and nearly fall over backward as I tried to move away from him.

Bastian had just growled.

"No," I said, my word given shape by the frozen air.

"Calla?" Bastian stepped toward me, his eyes questioning.

"Stay away!" I spun, keeping my body between him and my baby as much as possible while I fumbled with my keys. "Did Aaric send you? Because I'm not running. There's no reason to punish me."

"Calla, wait."

I swung open the door and climbed inside, slamming it shut and locking it behind me. Not that metal and glass would keep someone like him away, but in my mind, it was better than nothing. Shaking, I tried to start the engine, but it clicked and refused to turn over.

"C'mon, c'mon, c'mon." I tried again and again, but it was no use. My car wouldn't start. My eyes began to fill with tears, fear making my body shake in my seat.

"Calla, please." Bastian leaned down and knocked on the window. "Your battery's probably dead—"

"And I bet you had nothing to do with that, right?"

He placed a hand against the glass. "Of course not. I wouldn't trick you like that."

I snorted, fear quickly turning to anger. "Please, you've been playing me for a fool all night with your sweet little smiles and your kindness. You didn't have to be so fake with me; it's not like I would've told anyone what you are."

Bastian moved back, eyes wide enough to see even with how dark the parking lot was. "What do you mean?"

I snorted a scoff. "Tell Aaric next time he wants to deliver a message, he'd better do it himself. I'm not going to try to run away again, and I've never told anyone about his pack of wolf shifters. Now leave me alone!"

Beast

I STOOD IN THE freezing cold, staring at Calla through her car window with my mouth hanging open. Shocked was an understatement for how I felt—how could she possibly know what I was? She was human; she shouldn't be able to sense my shifter side.

But underneath that surprise was also a deluge of pain. My mate was afraid of me. She knew I was a shifter, and that terrified her. If I hadn't drugged my wolf spirit down to his current, nearly comatose levels, he'd be howling a mournful song in my head.

Unfortunately, the agony making my chest collapse in on itself would have to be ignored. Calla needed to be cared for first. Sniffing, reaching deep for any of my wolf senses I could wake, I searched out Calla's scent. Flowery—reminding me of the huge blossoms my mother grew beside our den when I was a child. She definitely wasn't a shifter—I would have sensed that from the first step into the diner. She did carry a light scent of wolf on her, though. Delicate, almost hidden under her human scent. A friend? Family member? Perhaps a lover? As much as I hated the thought of her with someone else, I couldn't ignore the fact that she had to have a man in her life. The baby in her belly had been conceived with a partner, and that partner could be another shifter.

Still, even if she was associated with another wolf, that didn't mean she should be able to tell I was a shifter as well. I'd barely growled at her when I jumped back, a noise most people would have put off as a grunt. Her question and willingness to touch the scarred side of my face had caught me off guard. Most people avoided the damaged parts of me; she seemed intrigued by them.

Taking a deep breath and willing myself to be patient and speak carefully, I squatted down and knocked on the window. I couldn't claim her as mine since she already belonged to another. I couldn't feed her or take care of her, either, as those responsibilities belonged to her chosen partner. But handling car repairs and making sure a pregnant woman got home safely? That I could do…if only she'd let me.

"Calla," I said, keeping my voice as even as I could. "Your car won't start, and I'm not leaving you in a dark parking lot in the cold without some plan for you to get home."

"No," she snapped, her eyes wild. "Just leave me alone."

I huffed, my temper fraying. "Why are you so afraid?"

"I know your kind." She met my eyes through the glass, hers filled with a fear that punched me in the gut.

"I'm not a *kind*," I said softly. "I'm just me…Bastian Martinez de Caballero. A mechanic from Michigan who wants to help you."

Her eyes filled with tears, her bottom lip quivering. "Please. I'm nine months pregnant. I just want to go home and keep my baby safe."

I nodded, warring with myself over whether to feel heartbroken at the sadness in her voice or rage at the wary way she regarded me. Someone had hurt her badly, obviously a fellow shifter.

"Okay, *cariño*," I said, the endearment my father had called my mother rolling off my tongue with ease. "I'll make sure you and your precious angel get home safely. I promise. But to do that, you're going to have to trust me enough to at least open the door."

She edged away. "Why?"

"Because to get you home, either you need to call someone for help or I'm going to have to drive you. I assume you don't have a phone or else you'd already be calling nine-one-one."

She shook her head. "I don't have a cell phone."

I pulled my phone from my pocket and held it up. "You can borrow mine if you'd like. You don't even have to open the door; just roll the window down a bit and I'll push it through." When her tears began to fall, I leaned forward, ready to claw through the damned door separating us.

"Calla, I swear to every god anyone has ever prayed to, I will not hurt you. Let me help get you home and out of this cold."

She swallowed hard and wiped at the tears tracking down her cheeks. "I have no one to call."

I growled, wanting to pound my fists into the concrete. Where was the father of her child? Who was making sure she was protected and cared for? Pregnant women were vulnerable, their bodies working hard to produce a little miracle at their own expense. My mate was exhausted—her tired eyes proof enough of that. She worked far too hard for someone so far along in her pregnancy. She needed more rest, more time off her feet, and for someone to put her first. My father treated my mother like a queen most of the time, but especially when she was pregnant with my sister. That was the man's job as mate.

Sighing, I dropped my head, forcing down the pull of the mating bond and doing my best to remember that I was dealing with a woman who had chosen another to live her life with.

"I'm trying to do the right thing here, Calla," I said, looking up to meet her frightened gaze, wishing for more than I could have. "Please, let's move this conversation to my truck, which starts and has heat. Let me take you home."

She stared at me through the glass for a long time, sizing me up. I truly thought she'd turn me down and I'd be forced to give her my keys so she could drive herself home, but then she huffed and opened her door. "My neighbor knows what time my shift ends and is nosy. If I don't make it home, she'll call the cops."

I nodded and held out my hand as I rose to my feet, relief making me feel lighter than before. "Noted. But you can trust me. Just let me take care of you"—I blanched, the words hitting too close to home—"for the night. Let me get you home and make sure you two are safe."

She shook her head, the strangest look appearing in her eyes. "Why would you even bother?"

I shrugged, playing casual. "Because my father taught me to be a gentleman, and occasionally I like to remind myself of that."

She frowned as if she thought my answer wasn't truthful but still followed me to my truck, her footsteps slow and wary across the snow-covered pavement. Once there, I helped her up into the seat and hurried around to the driver's side so I could start the engine. The behemoth vehicle heated up fast, which was a good thing. Standing beside her car for ten minutes arguing had made my balls nearly tuck themselves inside my body.

Once the engine was warm and Calla stopped shivering, I put the truck in gear. "Where to?"

She pointed to the left. A few twists and turns later, and she had me pulling up to what had to be a low-income apartment home. The entire place looked dilapidated, even in the dark of night. Cracked sidewalks that obviously hadn't been shoveled for a snowstorm or two, no working lights in the parking lot, and a sagging roofline spoke clearly of neglect.

When I turned off the engine, her head whipped in my direction.

"What are you doing?"

"I told you I'd make sure you got home safely." I pointed, indicating the open hallways and exposed doors that meant she wouldn't be safe until she was actually inside her apartment. "You have no outer door to the building, which means you're outside. Getting you home safely means to your door."

Calla didn't argue. Instead, she huffed and threw open her door before dropping to the ground below. I bit back a smile at her antics. My mate had a sass that I found irresistible. And didn't that thought just bite me in the ass? She was my mate, made by the fates to be the perfect partner for me, but I couldn't have her. She'd probably have run me ragged with her attitude and spunk, and I would have loved every minute of it. Like Rebel and the way he was with his mate, Charlotte. That woman had a power over him few men would put up with, but Rebel took it all with a smile and an air of complete happiness. Lucky fucker.

I followed Calla up the stairs and along the concrete walkway to a door on the second floor. She unlocked the cheap handle and stepped inside, pausing to give me a look that almost made me take a step back. Attitude indeed.

"I'm home," she said, walking farther into the apartment but leaving the door open.

"Then my work here is done." I yawned, exhaustion still weighing me down, but that open door looked awfully tempting.

Knowing it was wrong but too curious to pass the opportunity by, I stepped inside and shut the door behind me. The place was a dump, though it was tidy and clean. The windows were covered with blankets, obviously trying to block a draft. The small kitchen to my right looked as if it hadn't been updated in at least forty years, and the carpet was worn clear through in places. But it smelled clean and it glowed with a homey warmth. I liked it. Probably more than I should have.

Calla watched me for a moment as she removed her coat and gloves, her eyes a lot less wary than back at the diner. Perhaps more comfortable in her own space. I suddenly wished I was Draught-free, that I could use my wolf senses to their full abilities. Especially my nose. I wanted to scent my mate. To absorb her into my memories so that later, when I'd gone back home so she could live her life with her chosen partner, well…

"Would you like a cup of coffee before you go?" she asked, surprising me with her offer. "I usually make a small pot of decaf when I get home."

I shook my head, smiling as those walls around her showed their first signs of weakness. "No, but thank you. I wouldn't want to invade your space."

She huffed a laugh. "Invade away. There's not much here, really." She walked into the little kitchen, leaving me alone by the door. I wasn't going to stay, but when she opened her refrigerator, my protective instincts swelled. There was no food. Condiments, a couple of apples, and a pack of what looked like hot dogs were all I could see. My mate had almost nothing to eat.

It took me less than a second to unzip my coat. Calla was in trouble, but I had no idea how much. The shifters, the fear, the lack of food—I needed to learn more about her so I could help get her someplace safe and make sure she could eat. No wonder she looked so tired.

Sniffing subtly, digging deep in the hope of rousing my drugged wolf spirit, I searched for any input on her life. Sadly, my wolf was down for the count. Still, my senses were stronger than any human's, even with the lack of wolf participation. Walking in a circle, I concentrated on my nose. I didn't notice a strong scent of another man in the place. No other people at all, in fact. Just Calla and that wolf scent she carried on her.

Pictures hung on a corkboard in the living room, catching my eye. I focused on those as Calla moved about the kitchen. Each one was a moment of her life, plenty from what looked like her teenaged years, a few of an older couple who could have been her grandparents, and a handful of black and white printed shots of what must have been the little baby in her belly. Tiny, helpless, and completely captivating, the way the pictures showed the progress from blob to what was obviously a curled-up child made my heart nearly break with want and loss.

"Where's her father?" The words came out before I could stop them, my curiosity definitely piqued by the lack of men in the pictures.

Calla snorted. "You mean you don't know him?"

"Know who?"

"I figured all you shifters knew each other. Aaric used to be able to tell exactly who'd been in the diner by the smell of them on me."

"I'm not from around here. I don't know anyone locally." I glanced at her over my shoulder and grinned. "Except for you."

"Hmmm." She moved to the couch and sat down slowly, her hand supporting her weight during the descent. "The father, Aaric, lives out with the pack. He's not really involved in my life at the moment."

"He doesn't help you?"

"No. But I don't need anyone's help. We're doing just fine."

"Gotcha." I nodded, thinking how much better she could be doing if she could truly be mine. This Aaric must have been a fool, or too tied up in pack politics to be brave enough to fight for his woman. Some packs had rules against bringing unmated humans into the group, but she carried his child. If I had been lucky enough to be Aaric, I would have challenged any wolf who stood in my way to keep Calla at my side. Of course, she actually *was* my mate…she would have been welcomed in any pack as such.

I must have been too quiet, trapped in my own thoughts for too long, because her next whisper caught me off guard.

"I'm not stupid."

I spun, surprised not just by her words but by the way she said them. The defeat in her tone. "I never assumed you were."

"Well, you'd be the only one in this town." She dropped her gaze to the floor. "I thought he really cared for me. There was no way I could've known he'd change so much. He said I was…"

I cocked my head, waiting for more. When it didn't come, I prompted, "He said you were what?"

She shook her head and shrugged, her eyes not meeting mine. "He said I was meant to be his."

My heart cracked, a deep, burning pain that only served to fuel my rage. He had her, and he didn't appreciate her. I would've died for her, but I couldn't let her know. The defeat was agonizing.

"He said he cared," I whispered, moving a step closer. "And you trusted him at his word."

Calla sniffed and nodded. "But then I got pregnant, and he stopped being so nice. He threw an absolute fit when I refused to move with him onto pack land."

I took a deep breath, fighting back the need to punch a wall, something to release the frustration and anger building inside of me at the way Calla had been treated. But the comment about not living on pack land made me pause.

"Why didn't you want to be with the pack?"

"I didn't want to be around those animals." She looked up, fear written across her face. "I didn't mean it like…you seem much more… I don't know why I'm telling you all this."

"Because I'm here." I smiled, not putting too much stock in her comment about the pack wolves since I didn't see myself as one. "And maybe because you needed someone to talk to."

Calla stared for a long moment, disbelieving. And then her face fell along with her gaze.

"Yeah, well, talk won't keep the lights on." She shuffled forward, leaning to the side so she could push herself off the couch. I hurried to her, my heart jumping as she grabbed the hand I'd offered to help her up. Gently, carefully, I guided her to her feet, holding her hand like it was something precious and breakable. Which it was, at least to me.

"Thanks for the ride and for listening to me complain," Calla said once she was on her feet. "No offense, but I need to get some sleep, so I think it's time for you to go."

"Of course." My heart lay heavy in my chest as I walked toward the door. I didn't want to leave her just yet. I had so many questions, so many things I needed to work out so I could help her before I could let her go. But she needed rest; that was obvious. In an act of desperation, I grabbed a pen and a piece of paper off the table and scribbled my cell phone number down.

"If you need anything, please call me." I handed her the slip of paper, watching as she looked down at the numbers scrawled in blue. "I mean it, Calla. Anything at all. I'll be in town for a few days at least."

"The only phone I have access to is the one at the diner." She smiled halfheartedly, tucking the slip of paper in her back pocket. "But sure; I'll call if I need something."

Resigned to leave, I quickly slid into my coat and opened the door, looking back one more time before I left her for the night. "Thank you for inviting me into your home."

She looked surprised as she replied, "You're welcome."

Giving her one final smile, I turned and tore myself from the warmth of her presence. The wind screamed through the open hall, making me curl into the collar of my coat. I trudged down the stairs, my heart heavy in my chest at the thought of leaving my mate behind. She needed help, needed more than what she had, but I still wasn't sure what the situation was between her and the fucker who'd fathered her child. It seemed precarious at the least, but I didn't want to get my hopes up. They were having a child together; a baby could calm whatever storm brewed between them.

Back at the hotel, I tossed my jacket on the chair and headed straight for the bathroom. Fuck, I'd been hard all night. Her eyes, her smile, the way her pale skin nearly glowed in the shadows behind the diner. Like an angel. I'd foolishly thought she'd felt the mating pull at the diner, had let myself hope for more than just a friendly conversation. And while helping her out of a tough situation would technically be more, I'd fallen into the trap of wanting *more*. If I were being honest with myself, I'd let myself hope for everything, which made getting nothing even harder to take.

*She is a claimed woman.*

Sighing, I turned the water on and stripped out of my clothes, fisting my heavy cock as soon as I dropped my jeans. I couldn't help myself. She'd touched me voluntarily in the parking lot. True, it'd made me jump, but she'd not been afraid or disgusted by my face. She'd *seen* me and moved closer instead of backing away.

That thought—and the reminder of the way her hips swayed when she walked—had my hand sliding up and down my cock in quick strokes the second I stepped in the shower. The act was wrong on so many levels, and yet it felt so right. I placed my other hand against the wall and dropped my head under the hot water, enjoying the tingles beginning in my gut. Calla was gorgeous, kind, and so fucking strong. Independent. A good mate for a man like me.

I growled as my hand moved faster, my thumb sliding over the tip every few passes, the pressure tweaking the titanium frenum just under the head. She was supposed to be mine, but she wasn't. She was my only one—there would be no other for me—but I couldn't let her know. Damn it! I gripped myself tighter, making it hurt, reveling in the pain as my growls turned to a snarl. Never enough. Nothing I did was ever enough. I would always pay for the mistakes I'd made. I would never be good enough to get—

Calla's sweet smile faded into my thoughts, pulling me from my internal ranting. As my balls tightened and my gut clenched, I made myself a promise to do right by her. To make sure she was taken care of before I left.

A moan, a growl, and one final tug was all it took for me to come against the tile wall. Spent. Exhausted. The tiredness of my body catching up to me.

Stepping out of the shower, I dried off but I didn't fall into bed. Instead, I redressed. My skin itched and my mind was too on edge to sleep.

*"Who are you hiding under there?"*

I met my own eyes in the mirror, seeing myself as Calla would. The ink that covered my arms and peeked over the edge of my collar. The thick beard that darkened the lower half of my face. The scars I'd lived with for most of my life. Was I hiding? I didn't think so, but my mate did. So maybe…

Without giving myself time to overthink my actions, I reached for my toiletries bag. It banged against the sink, heavy from all the crap I'd brought with me. I'd tossed shit in the leather bag assuming I'd be gone for a while, not planning to do what I was about to do. But my mate thought I was hiding, and she was the one person I'd never want to hide from.

A half hour later, I ran my hand over my jaw and chin. My cleanly shaven jaw and chin. I hadn't been without my beard in well over a hundred years. I felt oddly naked, and yet the scarred and rugged face staring back at me filled me with pride. This would make my mate happy.

After putting away my clippers and razor and cleaning up the mess in the sink, I paced the room, restless. My mate was alone. Her fear in the back parking lot of the diner had been real, which told me she'd been hurt before and very likely by another shifter. If one of my kind showed up at her apartment, she'd be no match for his strength and speed, especially with her being so far along in her pregnancy. Calla may not want me close, but I couldn't leave her and her baby unprotected. I'd go back and watch over her…over the two of them.

*My girls.*

I shoved that thought back, because the truth was they weren't my girls. They were his girls…Aaric's girls. And while I didn't want to appear to be some kind of crazy stalker, my mate and her unborn child needed looking after. If Calla and Aaric's current relationship struggles kept him from living up to those needs, I'd step in. I may not be able to replace him in her life, but I could swoop in and make sure she and her little family were taken care of while I was here.

It was the least I could do.

# SIX

*Calla*

I STARED IN THE refrigerator as my stomach growled, hating myself a little bit for being so forgetful. I hadn't picked up milk at the gas station, which meant no cereal or pancakes for breakfast. I bit my lip as a massive craving for dairy wrapped its barbed bands around me. If I had my car, I could run to the grocery store and grab a gallon, but I'd left it behind the diner. I had no milk for my breakfast, no car to get milk, and no way to get to work. Not my brightest move by far.

Not that the car thing was my fault, but still. I probably should've called the tow truck to give me a jump like last time. I hated the thought of spending the fifty dollars it would've cost me, but then I wouldn't be in this situation. Hungry, craving something I didn't have, and with no way to acquire what I wanted. Darn that Bastian and his crooked smile. If it had been anyone else, I would have waved them off and paid to have my car jumped. But last night, that man… I shivered thinking about the attraction I'd felt to him. How kind he'd been. How much I wanted to be…*something* to him.

But he was a wolf shifter, like Aaric and his pack. And though he didn't scare me as much as the others did, it was still difficult for me to imagine trusting him. I'd let him into my home, though, which still surprised me. I'd told him about Aaric, a double surprise. But when I was around Bastian, it was as if everything was going to be okay. I was safe with him; he'd protect me from the demons at my door. Or so I thought. I had no proof he'd do anything more than join in when the pack came for me. He could use his claws against me the same way Aaric did, or overpower me the way the rest of the pack had.

My fingers traced the scars on my legs, the slashes right down the center of my thighs. Claw marks. Reminders of the truth about shifters. No matter how sweet Bastian seemed, or how safe he made me feel, he was still an animal inside. One I'd be better off avoiding.

I was about to put a couple of slices of stale bread in the toaster for a simple breakfast when someone knocked on my door. I hurried across the room, worried my elderly neighbor Mrs. Frank needed something. I hadn't been kidding when I'd told Bastian about my nosy neighbor—Mrs. Frank had probably seen Bastian come and go. Even if she didn't need anything, I figured she'd be showing up for coffee and gossip. But it wasn't Mrs. Frank on the other side. Not even close.

Bastian stood in my doorway, collar of his leather coat pulled up against the wind, a gray scarf wrapped around his throat and tucked inside. And no beard in sight. I stared, unable to form words. He looked like a model. Rugged and dangerous with his scars, but still gorgeous. And he was carrying grocery bags.

"Good morning," he said with a nod. I stood stock-still, staring, my mind stuck.

Looking decidedly uncomfortable, he shifted his feet and lifted a single shoulder in a shrug. "I worried you might be stuck without your car, so I brought a few things for breakfast. I can just…"

He moved as if to set the bags down inside the threshold, a motion that managed to unstick my brain.

"Sorry," I huffed as I opened the door wider. "I'm just surprised to see you." I stepped back and indicated he should come inside.

"I didn't mean to intrude." He walked inside, immediately heading for the kitchen. "Last night when I left, I noticed there aren't a lot of businesses that are walkable for you, so I figured I'd better get up this morning and make sure you didn't need anything before work." He stopped unloading groceries, glaring at the counter. "Though I guess that was pretty presumptuous of me. I don't even know when you work or if you need a ride or—"

"It's fine," I interrupted. "Thanks for thinking of me. That was very kind."

"Oh," he whispered, his lips pulling up in the smile that made my heart flutter. "Good. Okay."

Confident and sure, he moved about my kitchen, placing baked goods and fruit on the little counter by the sink. He filled my refrigerator shelves with meats and cheeses, fresh fruits and vegetables. Pastas and rice went into the cabinet, frozen dinners of the expensive organic kind in the freezer. More food than I'd ever been able to buy at one time, all loaded into my kitchen by a man I'd only just met.

None of that mattered, though, when he pulled a gallon of milk from the second bag.

"Oh, thank God!" I said as I nearly lunged for him.

Bastian looked up at me, a surprised expression on his ridiculously handsome face. "Want some milk, *cariño*?"

"Yes." I hurried to the cupboard to grab a glass, my face burning. "I'm not usually this excited about dairy products, but I woke up with a huge craving for milk. You're a life-saver right now."

His lips twitched as if fighting back a smile, his eyes practically sparkling. "I'm glad I could be of service."

Eyeing the eggs and bacon Bastian had brought, I took

a deep breath and tucked my fears away. Yes, he was a wolf shifter. Yes, he was inherently dangerous. But I'd felt no fear around him until I knew of his dual nature. I liked him, felt an attraction to him even, and I needed to say thank you.

"Would you like to stay for breakfast?" I asked, my voice small and quiet. Bastian's head jerked, his eyes meeting mine.

"I don't have to stay if you don't want me to," he said, his voice soft. "I can come back when it's time for you to go to work and give you a lift."

I stared, the moment tense and heavy. This was about so much more than breakfast, but I wasn't ready to examine the what or why of the moment. Instead, I let my heart and my gut be the catalyst for my decisions, keeping any negative thoughts under lock and key.

"I'd like for you to stay."

His smile bloomed bright and slow, making the skin around his blue eyes crinkle in a way that spoke of years of experience and knowledge. He reached up, unwinding his scarf and pulling it over his head before pulling down the zipper on his leather coat, never breaking eye contact with me. And when his coat was off, when he stood before me in another long-sleeved T-shirt that stretched across his muscled chest and accented the strength in his arms, he leaned down to place a tiny kiss on my cheek.

"Whatever you'd like, *cariño*."

Twenty minutes later, the two of us sat on the floor, eating off plates set on the coffee table. The apartment wasn't big enough for a dining room set, not that I had the money to buy one anyway. I was used to the odd eating situation, but my face burned when I told Bastian where he could sit. Not that he said anything. He simply strolled across the room and sat down, crossing his legs like a child at story time.

"So," I asked as I picked up my last piece of bacon. "Why'd you do it?"

Bastian's eyebrows drew together. "Do what?"

I pointed at his chin. "Why'd you shave your beard?"

His cheeks darkened, and he went back to staring at his plate, an irresistible show of charming shyness from such a beast of a man.

"I, uh…heard what you said." He looked up, eyes serious as they met mine. "I didn't want to hide—not from you—so I shaved it off."

My world tilted, the man's sweet words making me want to be near him. To crawl into his lap and feel those muscles envelop me. To be surrounded and wholly held by him.

"Thank you for letting me see the real you," I said, my voice quiet, my heart banging in my chest. "I didn't expect you to make such a big change."

He shrugged, the intensity in his eyes belying his forced casualness. "Yeah, well…this was easy. Just don't ask me to get my ink removed."

I snorted a laugh as he chuckled. "Never. I like the pretty pictures on your skin."

I ran a finger over his wrist, just as I had the night before. Bastian sighed softly at my touch, turning his hand over so his fingertips could rest on my arm as I followed the inked flourishes. Simple touches, the kind a stranger might be able to get away with, but the attraction between us was anything but simple. His eyes on mine, pupils wide. My fingers on his skin, stroking slow. We leaned into one another, the tension between us growing thick and heavy. I licked my bottom lip. He tracked the movement, mimicking me, the pink tip of his tongue gliding along his full lower lip. I suddenly wanted to feel his lips against mine, to know what he tasted like. To bite and lick and kiss him until the world went away and it was only he and I.

But a solid kick to my rib cage made that thought scatter. Startled by the pain, I jumped and hissed as my hand flew to my side.

"Apparently she's awake." Bastian smiled, his eyes serious when they met mine once more. He turned his hand over, weaving our fingers together as he moved them toward my stomach. "May I?"

I nodded, suddenly nervous. My belly was a huge issue. I was pregnant with another man's baby. It wasn't the best time to try to start anything with someone else. Besides, Aaric would probably kill him or me if he found out Bastian had even been in my apartment. This was a bad idea all the way around.

And yet, when our joined hands finally rested on the curve of my stomach, all the worry melted away. Bastian was gentle but obviously intrigued. His eyes were glued to where his hand met my stomach. I pushed down, smiling when he tried to pull away.

"It doesn't hurt." I pushed again, waiting for my little angel to respond. This was a game we played every day. Mommy pushed, baby kicked. And while I was selfish with her attention, having been the only person to experience a single kick from my child, I had a sudden desire to share the moment with Bastian. To bring him into our world. I pushed a third time, and the baby responded with a mighty kick, our hands bouncing a bit against my skin. Bastian's head whipped up, his eyes wide and his smile huge.

"She's strong," he whispered, amazement clear in his voice. My eyes burned as my smile grew. This…a moment like this was what I'd dreamed of when I first found out I was pregnant. But in those dreams, it was Aaric feeling the baby kick, being amazed by her rolls and flutters. When I'd ended my relationship with Aaric, I thought I'd never get to experience a moment like this one. But here I was—with Bastian—and his eyes were as bright as I would have expected a father's to be.

Staring at the place where my daughter had kicked, Bastian leaned forward. He whispered against the side of my stomach, words in a language I couldn't understand. Soft words that lilted and sang, rolling from his tongue in gentle waves. Waves my daughter seemed to like as much as I did. The baby moved and kicked, responding to him, making the moment even more special.

"I think she likes the sound of your voice." I grinned when he looked up at me, our fingers still twined together. "What were you saying to her?"

"It's a secret, just for her and me." Bastian sat up, giving my hand one more squeeze before he pulled it away. His expression turned serious, almost wary. "Where's the father of your baby, Calla? Why are you alone here?"

I pulled away from him, grabbing the dishes from the table to clean up. "You don't need to hear my sob story."

Bastian caught my elbow, halting my escape. "I realize we just met, but I want to know about you. That little girl is a part of you, which makes me want to know about her as well."

I shook my head, pulling my arm from his hold. As much as I wanted to open up to him, I couldn't. Or wouldn't, I guess. Aaric would kill me if he knew I'd told someone about our situation.

As I tried to back away, Bastian rose to his knees, so tall, his face was almost on the same level as mine even as I stood. He didn't try to grab me or hold me in place; he just knelt on the floor, imploring me with his eyes and his words.

"Trust me, Calla."

I closed my eyes, fighting back tears. Oh Lord, how I wanted to trust him. My heart already did, but my mind... Well, my mind held me back. I'd trusted someone when they told me to and gotten burned. I didn't think I could do it again.

When I opened my eyes, my gaze fell upon Bastian's scars. The extent of the damage more visible now without a beard to hide the scarring along his jaw and neck. He'd been brave enough to remove his armor for me; I wished I could do the same.

Taking the dirty plates from my hands and setting them behind me, Bastian sighed. "I know you don't trust shifters, but I'm not the one who came before me. I'm not here to trick you or hurt you. I just…feel drawn to you."

I nodded, feeling the same. Bastian's gaze held mine as he grabbed my hand, leading me closer. I stepped lightly, my movements slow and measured, fear and need and desire tangling together to make me unsure of my actions. Bastian seemed to understand my hesitancy. He never tugged or forced me to move at his speed. Instead, he kept a constant pressure on my hand, making the move my choice.

And I chose to step right into his embrace.

He pulled me into his arms, wrapping them around my hips. Warmth and comfort enveloped me, making me sigh and hold tight to him. And for the first time in a number of years, I felt at home.

"Put a little faith in me, Calla. I promise I won't let you down."

Clinging to his arms, I nodded and whispered a soft "I know." And I did know; I trusted this man more than I'd trusted anyone. At least my heart did. Something about him made me comfortable in ways I'd never experienced, and I knew I was safe with him.

Suddenly wanting him to know about my situation, I tried to organize my memories. There was so much that led to the child I was carrying. Months of manipulation and lies, of broken promises and abuse. Not all my time with Aaric had been bad, though. Our first few months together had been good, and I'd believed him when he'd said he cared about me. But in the end, the only thing he cared about was the one thing I hadn't given him. Yet.

Bastian pulled back, looking up at me. Willing me to put my faith in him. I'd prayed for someone to come help me, and here was a man on his knees, offering his help, wanting to get to know me. Divine intervention or one heck of a coincidence?

"Trust me, Calla. Tell me."

# SEVEN



THE SADNESS IN HER eyes gutted me, made me feel like less of a man for not being able to ease her suffering. She looked so fragile, so worn and weary. The woman before me appeared to have aged ten years in the last few minutes.

"I didn't know," she whispered. "When I met him, I didn't have any idea he wasn't…human."

I gave her a single head nod, letting her know everything was okay. That I was listening. When she took a deep breath and wobbled a bit, my protective urges took over. Jumping to my feet, I gripped her arms and directed her to the couch, doing my best to help her keep her balance. She curled up in the corner, completely defensive in her body language, her eyes refusing to meet mine. I grabbed the blanket from the back of the chair and covered her, needing her to feel warm and safe. And then I sat on the floor directly in front of her, guarding her as best I could.

"He was really nice to me when I first came here," she murmured, her fingers worrying the edge of the blanket. "I thought working for the oil companies would be my chance for a better career, a better life. I met Aaric right away, and things between us moved really fast. I believed him when he told me he loved me, and I trusted him when he said I was meant to be his. When I got pregnant, I thought the worst he could do was run, you know?" She looked up at me, her eyes filling with tears. I didn't know…couldn't imagine not wanting to be involved in my child's life, but I nodded anyway.

"He didn't run." Calla rubbed her leg as her eyes focused on something I couldn't see. "He went from being sweet and kind to demanding and obsessive. Everything was my fault. Everything I did was suddenly wrong. I lost my job when the company switched hands, and Aaric blamed me for it. Told me I was leeching off him and his pack. But when I got the job at the diner, he exploded. He saw it as making him look bad, as if he couldn't take care of me. But I didn't need anyone to take care of me. I could work, and I wanted to. He tried to make me quit, so I threatened to leave and go back to Minnesota. That's when he got violent with me."

She looked at me as her hand moved to cover her belly, shame evident on her face. "After the first time, I tried to get away. But I didn't even make it across town before he ran me off the road and punished me for it. I tried again a few times, but his pack never let me get too far. They'd catch me, threaten to hurt me, but Aaric would always rein them back in and handle my punishments himself. I thought it was an act, that the other wolves were just doing it to scare me. Until the last time."

I swallowed, fear and rage making my voice thick as I asked, "What happened the last time?"

She shook her head, her eyes bright with unshed tears. "You must think I'm the stupidest woman ever."

"Not at all."

Her eyes met mine, filled with disbelief. "How can you not? I knew better than to rely on him. I could have done so many things differently. 'Never need a man,' my grandma always said. 'You can want one with you, but never need one. They'll just let you down.'" She wiped away the tears that had finally begun to fall. "I should have listened to her more."

"You're not stupid, *cariño*. Believing a liar doesn't make you the bad guy." I reached for her hand, tentative and slow. There was nothing I could say to convince her, no words I could offer. But I could hold her hand and listen.

Thankfully, Calla didn't pull away. I wrapped my larger hand around her smaller one, hating the fact that my skin was so rough against hers. But she didn't seem to mind. She clung to me, hopefully taking strength from my touch.

After a deep breath, Calla whispered, "Aaric didn't love me; he only wanted to have a child with me. A daughter, specifically. He wants my baby, and then he'll pay for me to relocate. Set me up somewhere nice to start over. But I'd have to leave the baby behind."

The growl that rolled up from the pits of my soul caught in my throat, my rage burning bright behind it. "And are you going to—"

"I won't leave my baby," she spat, her eyes hard and filled with fury. "Not ever, not with anyone. I'd rather die first."

I nodded, relieved, and let my head fall back, my eyes following a pattern of cracks in the ceiling as I worked out logistics in my head. If I were being honest with myself, her story had actually given me a massive swell of hope. She wasn't tied to another. She wasn't claimed. If I could just earn her trust, I could reveal myself as her mate and offer her a better life. I could take care of her and her child. I could have my mate.

But Aaric had also told her he cared about her, and I had no idea how to explain the particulars of that situation. *Sure, he told you he's your mate, but really I am. Yep, he promised to take care of you and lied, but now I'm promising and I won't lie. I swear it.*

Fuck, words weren't going to work. I was going to have to

do something more…find a way to prove myself.

"So we leave," I said, as if it was the simplest and most logical answer.

Calla's eyes grew wide. "Excuse me?"

"You pack, I drive, done. I'll take you back to Detroit with me until the baby's born. Then we can decide what to do next."

She pulled her hand out of my hold. "You're crazy."

"No, I'm offering my help and giving you a way out of this situation." I rose to my knees, leaning over the edge of the couch and looking her square in the eyes. "Come with me."

"I can't." She shook her head. "There's no way."

"Why can't you?"

"Because he'll find me."

"Let him try," I growled.

Calla's eyes grew wider, her neck flushing. "You don't understand. He'll come for this baby. She's all he wants."

This time, I snarled, my lips pulling back over my teeth. "No one will be coming after that baby. Ever. If he dares to try, my friends and I will take care of it. Besides, you'd be hidden. He doesn't know anything about me or where I'm from."

"He'll track me."

I scoffed. "No wolf is that good of a hunter."

Her eyes softened as she leaned forward, our faces mere inches apart. "I appreciate the offer, but you don't understand. I didn't tell you everything. You don't know how trapped I really am."

"Then explain it to me," I whispered, reclaiming her hand. "Tell me how he could find you if you ran with me."

She closed her eyes and turned her face away, hiding from me. "Because he can sense me no matter where I go."

She paused, a long stretch of silence weighted down with anticipatory tension. And then she pulled the world as I knew it right out from underneath me.

"I'm his fated mate."

# EIGHT

*Calla*

BASTIAN'S FACE WENT SLACK and his eyes changed, turning so blue, they almost glowed. Like Aaric's did when he was becoming more wolf than man. But this was Bastian. He didn't scare me the way Aaric and his goons did. Whether it was the calm way he sat at my feet or the simple fact that it was *Bastian*, I didn't know. But I felt safe, even as his wolf showed himself.

I brought my knees to my chest and waited for him to say something…anything. Aaric had explained the whole mating business to me, how we were tied together forever. How there was no escaping his hold on me. Bastian had to know what that meant as well, which I assumed was why he couldn't speak.

The wait lasted longer than I would have thought, Bastian's eyes growing brighter and lighter with each passing minute. And then he growled, long and deep and extremely loud.

"He told you *what?*"

My brows furrowed as I watched him, the growl in his voice finally making my heart speed up. Apparently his wolf did scare me, at least a little.

"Aaric said we're mates. He can track me anywhere because

he senses me due to our bond."

Bastian closed his eyes, his nostrils flaring as he took a deep breath. "You're not his mate."

"What?" I asked, confused. "Of course I am; he's tracked me every time I've run. He knows where I am all the time. Do they not teach every shifter about mates?"

Bastian snorted and turned away, anger clear in his expression. "I know all about fated mates, Calla. What no one taught me was how shifters could be so dishonest and manipulative regarding such a sacred gift."

"What do you mean?"

He turned back, meeting my gaze. "What time do you work?"

The sudden change in subject left me reeling, and I took longer to answer than I should have as the words scattered in my mind. Finally, I whispered, "I start at two."

Bastian pulled a phone out of his pocket and glanced at the screen. "It's ten now. I need to make a few calls and figure out what's what with your car so I can get parts before your shift starts."

He stood, not meeting my gaze. As he turned toward the door, my stomach plummeted. He was running. Not that I blamed him; the thought of being irrevocably linked to someone as cruel as Aaric made me want to run as well. I'd tried numerous times and paid the price when his pack inevitably found me. But the fact that Bastian was leaving after I opened up to him stung, even though I could understand why he'd do it.

"Don't worry about me." I got up and walked into the kitchen to hide under the pretense of washing dishes. "I can handle my own problems."

I stood at the sink and waited for the final close of the door. Waited for the man to walk away from me and not come back. And though I'd only just met him, the thought of never seeing him again made me want to curl up and cry. In fact, my eyes were burning with the coming tears. I needed a few more moments, a few seconds so he could make his escape before I broke. I just needed—

"*Cariño*." His voice came from over my shoulder, as if he were standing directly behind me. I squeezed my eyes closed harder, fighting the imaginings of how warm his body would be pressed against mine. How safe and secure I'd felt in his arms. But this man wasn't my savior or the answer to my prayers. He was just a man, one who happened to turn into a wolf. One who was about to run away from the danger I'd gotten myself into.

"I get it," I murmured, crossing my arms over my chest. "I hold nothing against you. This situation is my doing, and I'll handle it. You just go."

"Calla—"

"I need to use the restroom." I spun past him, heading for the bathroom at the end of the hall, hoping to make it behind closed doors before the tears fell. "Just let yourself out."

But Bastian didn't let me go. His hand, so big and rough, gently grabbed my elbow, forcing me to turn his way. When his eyes met mine, there was no fear there, no pity. Just an openness and an honesty that made him even more attractive to me. And made my heart ache with a desire for things I knew I couldn't have.

"I'm not running." He held my gaze, crouching to look me square in the face. "I'm mad as hell about the lies this Aaric told you, and I don't want to scare you by seeing me this way. Besides, I need to lay some groundwork to get you out of here, and I really do want to fix your car. I hate the thought of you getting stuck somewhere without a way to call for help."

I nodded, unable to let myself believe him.

"I'm here to help you, Calla. Give me a little time to get everything in order, and then we'll get you out of here and to someplace safe." He pulled me close, his warm breath blowing across my lips as he said, "I will never leave you behind."

He closed his eyes and gave me a long, lingering kiss on the cheek. One that made my breath catch and my heart ache. With a squeeze of my arm and a look that burned with a desire I was probably imagining, he turned for the door. It took me a moment to catch my breath, to calm my racing heart enough to get my thoughts out.

"What are you?" I asked, my voice barely above a whisper. "Some kind of knight in shining armor?"

He slid into his coat and donned a knit cap. "Nope, I'm just a mechanic with a soft spot for brave women." He grinned, the happiness on his face taking me by surprise. "Go take care of what you need to while I do the same. I'll be here to pick you up before two."

I wrapped my arms around myself, scared to hope. "Really?"

His smile turned sweet. "Of course. I'm a man of my word, *cariño*. And I promise I will get you out of here." He stepped outside, but before he closed the door, he gave me a look filled with heat.

"And just so you know, that man is definitely not your mate."

# NINE



RUNNING TO MY TRUCK, I fought the urge to rip down the entire goddamned building.

*"He's my fated mate."*

My growl was uncontrollable, my wolf fighting through his haze. He'd come awake as soon as Calla had told me what that fucker Aaric had told her, how he'd lied. She was my mate, not his. Not anyone else's. And I was going to rip his fucking arms off once I woke my wolf all the way up and made sure Calla was safe.

Calla and the baby.

Feeling that little life moving inside of her had been a reality-shifting moment for me. I'd known right then that there was no way I could leave my mate behind. Fuck her relationship with the father. I wanted to be involved in Calla's and the baby's lives. I could claim Calla as my own, take care of her and her daughter. And I would, once I destroyed the pack that threatened them both.

As soon as I jumped in the truck, I grabbed my cell phone. I'd turned it on the second I'd given the number to Calla, immediately deleting all the texts and voicemails without reading or listening to them. I wasn't quite ready to deal with everything back home, but I needed backup. So I called the man I knew would do anything for me.

Gates answered on the second ring. "What's up, *mi hermano?*"

I closed my eyes, nearly sighing in relief at hearing that voice. Gates was my last remaining family member, and we'd been through hell together more times than I could count. There was no way he'd let me down.

"I need help, Lorenzo." The fact that I used his real name and not his road name probably shocked him, but it also would speak to the seriousness of my call. We were only Lorenzo and Bastian when the trouble was personal, and saving my mate's life was really fucking personal.

He was quiet for a few seconds, but then he spoke the words I knew he would.

"What can I do?"

"My mate's in trouble," I said, knowing the news of my even having a mate would be a surprise to him. But we could talk details once he got here. "I need an extraction team in place to get her out of here when she's ready."

"What's the delay?"

"She doesn't trust me. But she's in some kind of trouble, man." I pulled onto the highway, driving fast in the direction of the nearest relatively large town. I needed supplies.

Gates hummed, his strategical soldier mind probably kicking in with plans and options. "Can we snatch and grab? Beg for forgiveness later?"

"No, this fucker really did a number on her. If I lie or take her without her permission, I don't think she'll ever trust me again."

"She's human?"

"Yeah, so I have to be careful how I proceed."

"Anyone in particular you want?" he asked.

I sighed, the tension leaving my shoulders already. "Bring me Shadow, you, and Princess."

"I'll have to pick up Shadow on the way—he's still in Chicago with Blaze." Gates paused, and I knew why. Princess, or Kaija, was a new Feral Breed member, our first female. She was also his mate. "Why do you want Kaija?"

"Calla's pregnant," I said, knowing how much that fact would mean to him. The memories of the cabin burning in the desert were not mine alone. "If this goes south and we have to run, I want Shadow because he's a medic. But I have a feeling a woman would help as well…somehow."

A bang sounded in the background, something like a door slamming. "Text me your location. You know we'll be there, brother."

"I know," I said, truly understanding how much I was asking of him. "But thank you, especially for Kaija."

"No thanks needed. Besides, I'm pretty sure she's going to tackle you with hugs just for asking for her."

"Damn right I will," Kaija yelled in the background.

"Tell her I'll be waiting for her short ass to get here," I sighed, relief flooding through me. My team would be on their way soon, and then we could work together to help Calla and the baby.

"And hey, Bastian?" Gates said, his voice lighter than normal.

"Yeah?"

"Congratulations on finding your mate."

I grinned and gunned the engine. "Thanks, brother."


THE DRIVE TO THE auto parts store took longer than expected, and I was almost late picking Calla up for her shift. She still seemed a bit nervous around me—not quite ready to trust—but I couldn't blame her. I wouldn't trust a shifter either if I'd been manipulated the way she had. And that's exactly what this Aaric had done. He hadn't just lied or twisted the truth to get his way; he'd completely worked his way inside Calla's life and changed her through deceit. The fucker deserved pack justice…something dark and cruel to remind him of what honor and respect meant.

But before I could deal with him, I needed to get Calla and the baby the fuck out of town. She'd have to trust me to help her, though, and that was going to be a tough negotiation. One I didn't know if I could pull off.

By the time I got her to work and started taking apart her car, the sun was already setting. Not that it mattered much; between enhanced night vision and the fact that I'd been tinkering with combustion engines since the days before Henry Ford, replacing the starter and battery was basically an exercise in muscle memory.

I had just seated the battery into the box when the quiet behind the diner was interrupted by a shrill ringing sound. I pulled my phone from my pocket, smiling when I saw who was calling. Truth be told, I'd missed the little fire witch.

"What's up, Zippo?"

"Not too much. How're they hanging, tall, dark, and growly?"

"It's too fucking cold for them to be hanging anywhere right now." I leaned against the side of the truck, letting the vehicle block the wind. "How goes dating in the dirty D?"

Scarlett was quiet for a second, which wasn't like her at all. "I'm not really dating much. Just…trying things out."

I nodded, not sure what more to say on that. "Seriously, what's up, kid?"

"Eh, Amber said she was sensing a disturbance in the force in regards to you and was too afraid to call you herself."

I rolled my eyes skyward. "She needs to learn to mind her business."

"You do realize we're witches, right? And you're a wolf shifter with enhanced senses? Any veil of privacy has long been tossed out the window." She shushed someone in the background, probably Amber. "The sighted one's going nuts here. Spill it, Suzie Sunshine."

I sighed, watching the mist dance in the night air. "I met my mate."

Scarlett paused as if waiting for more. When none came, she coughed. "So apparently there's a caveat to that statement."

"She doesn't trust shifters." I closed my eyes. "And she's pregnant."

"Oof."

"Yeah, oof." I dropped my head forward, letting all the moments I'd spent with my mate wash over me. Those memories shored me up, making me want to fight for her. To be better for her.

Scarlett finally gave me a drawn out, "And…"

Fuck, I certainly wasn't having any luck solving my problems on my own. Maybe the fiery one could help.

Taking a deep breath and glaring into the woods, I said, "The kid's from a relationship with another wolf shifter. One who lied and told her she was his mate. Calla doesn't trust me and believes this guy will track her if she leaves."

"Can he do that?"

"No. Only true mates who've exchanged mating bites can sense one another that way."

"You are a freaky breed, my friend."

I sighed, giving up any pretense of pride. "Please," I whispered. "Give me three minutes of seriousness. What do I do?"

The silence from Scarlett felt weighted, as if she were truly giving my question thought instead of spouting off nonsense and sarcasm. When she finally did speak, her voice was deeper, more serious, her tone reflecting how important she felt her words were.

"Trust is hard-won and easily broken. It's delicate, and hers has been shattered. It's going to take some serious wooing to get her to come around and trust you. Especially with a child involved. Those protective mother instincts are a real bitch."

"No shit, Sherlock."

"I wasn't finished," she scolded. "Be direct, don't lie, don't pussyfoot. Remember that no matter what you say, your actions are going to speak louder than your words, so make sure you follow through. Tell her you're her mate, keep telling her, and worry about convincing her of that truth later." There was a mumble, as if a conversation was going on between her and Amber before she came back. "You have a little time, but not much. A couple of days at most. And Amber says whatever you do, don't let the shadows fall."

"What shadows?"

"Don't know…I'd tell you to ask the fortune-teller but she's wiped. Says you need to get on with the mating. Whatever she did gave her more insight into your situation than she cares to admit. I think you're overloading her brain."

"I'd apologize but I'm still pissed she fucked with me the way she did."

"Yeah, she feels bad about it, but sometimes the end justifies the means, you know? At least to her." Scarlett went silent once more, a feeling of tension coming through the receiver like I'd never experienced. And when she spoke again, her voice was filled with a meaning I couldn't understand.

"Don't fuck this up, Beast. Direct, open, honest…those are your goals. When people we love lie, it kills a little piece inside of us. You can tell her to trust you all you want, but the fact of the matter is the guy who broke her probably told her the same thing. Do better."

I was still thinking about Scarlett's words as a car pulled up beside me. A sense of danger whispered at me, too far buried under days on end of The Draught to be clear, so I quickly disconnected the call and eyed the newcomer warily. The man that stepped out was tall and thin, wearing a black wool coat that probably cost more than Calla made in a week. He was also a wolf; I could smell the shifter in him.

"Well hello," he said as he rounded the front of my truck. "I'm Aaric Reeves, Beta of the local pack."

# TEN

*Calla*

"SEE YOU TOMORROW, MANNIE." I rushed to the back hallway for my coat. This was new, this feeling of excitement to see someone. I tried to write it off as just a little crush, but Bastian made me feel safe and cared for, something Aaric never really did. Something that made me want my new friend in a lot of different ways.

I'd seen Bastian working on my car all afternoon and evening as I snuck breaks and peeked out the window in the door. Head down, leaning over the front, usually with a frown on his handsome face. And he was handsome…very much so. Handsome and kind, with honest eyes brighter than the sky. Excited and almost giddy, my hands shook as I zipped my coat and pulled on my hat. Bastian wasn't just handsome and sexy—though he was both in spades—he also gave me friendship. He gave me the possibility of options. He gave me hope.

I swung open the back door with a smile, but the grin quickly slid from my face. Bastian wasn't alone. He stood by my car with Aaric, talking. I watched for more than a moment as the two conversed. Even though I couldn't see Bastian's face, I could tell he was relaxed. Calm. As if he and Aaric were old friends.

My stomach plummeted. The fact that these men were of the same breed, wolf shifters, slammed hard into my chest. How many of them could there be? They had to know one another, had to have met before or at least know the same people. Oh God, Bastian had told me he wasn't from around here and so he didn't know anyone. Had he lied to me? Had I fallen for another man just like Aaric? What if Bastian was just leading me on—

"There's my girl." Aaric's saccharine voice broke me from my thoughts, forcing my feet into motion. I approached slowly, with caution, unsure if I was walking into some kind of trap.

Aaric leered at me, the smirk on his lips growing wider the closer I came. Bastian's face was still hidden, still looking in Aaric's direction. He didn't turn to greet me or acknowledge my presence, which made my stomach fall even further.

"How are you, sunshine?" Aaric leaned down, obviously aiming for a kiss, but I turned my head enough to avoid lip contact. I caught Bastian's eye as Aaric kissed my cheek. One and the same, the two of them. Both shifters. Both dangerous.

Bastian's eyes stared into mine intently, a look of determination on his face. But he didn't say anything, didn't step closer or make any move to reassure me. His actions screamed the truth—he was more concerned about Aaric than he was about me.

Uncomfortable under the scrutiny and wanting to escape the reach of two predators, I broke my gaze with Bastian and looked toward my car instead.

"I'm fine. Is my car ready?"

"Yeah. You're all set," Bastian said after a small pause, his voice a bit deeper and rougher than normal.

"Fabulous," Aaric said with a wicked smile. "Next time call me if you need help, Calla. I'd hate to think what could have happened if Beast here lived up to the reputation of his group."

I paused, the use of some kind of nickname going off in my head like a shot, like a warning. Aaric obviously knew more about Bastian than I did, and he wasn't about to let me get away without sharing those details. That thought terrified me because I knew whatever Aaric had to say about Bastian would be bad. I sensed it. Could feel the fall coming.

"He's a Feral Breed member," Aaric said, almost giddy as he ripped my heart out with his words. "They're the hired mutts of our proud shifter world. Tell me, Beast; is it true you're the brother to the Gatekeeper?"

The anxious confusion made my breath hard to catch, and I found myself staring at Bastian's blue eyes, willing him to look at me…to talk to me. Or Beast, apparently. Either way, his face was curved into what I could only explain as a glower, his eyes staying locked on Aaric. The man was pissed off, but was it at Aaric for busting his cover or at me for getting between him and whatever he and his friend were planning?

Bastian nodded once, stiff and angry, as Aaric's smile grew.

"Now there's a shifter to be wary of. He's killed more men than any Feral Breed member, from what my National Association of the Lycan Brotherhood regional head tells me. I wonder how many of them were human?"

My stomach dropped, and I was sure I was about to throw up all over Aaric's shoes. Bastian's brother was a murderer? Did that mean Bastian was as well?

"I don't know for sure," Bastian replied with a tight shrug. "Though I'm sure the president of the NALB has record of it somewhere. I'll ask next time I see Blaze. Oh wait, you pack wolves know him as Blasius, right?"

Aaric nodded, not looking happy. I glanced from one man to the other, feeling the tension between them. I had no idea what was going on here, though it felt as if they were tied up in some kind of pissing match or a territorial dispute. They were both part-wolf, after all.

"Well, if everything's okay here, I'll be going." Aaric turned and grabbed my arms, clamping down on me like a vise. "Next time, you call me or one of the guys. I'm sure they'd be more than happy to help you in exchange for a little attention. Some of the boys were just saying how much they missed your—how did they word it?—oh right, sweet ass."

My stomach heaved. I gasped for air, turning my face to the side and bringing a fist to my mouth. *Not the pack…not again.* I looked to Bastian for help, but his head was down, his shoulders stiff and his hands clenched into fists probably against the cold. My heart cracked at the realization that he didn't care as much as I'd wanted him to. Maybe the whole trust and safety thing had been only in my mind. Maybe he was just another animal like the rest of them.

"Nice to meet you, Beast." Aaric pushed past me, giving me a glare. "I assume I won't be seeing you again as your work here is through."

"Not quite yet, Aaric," Bastian replied. "I've got a couple more things to take care of before I get on the road again."

"I'll make sure to let my regional head know the Breed has been through the area," Aaric said as he reached his car.

"And I'll make sure the Cleaners come up this way on their next run. Make sure your pack doesn't need a little…thinning." Bastian pulled his lips back, exposing his teeth. It turned his face from beautiful to evil, from man to animal. Disguise to truth.

When Aaric slammed his door and peeled out of his spot, Bastian dropped the expression. "Arrogant little fucker."

I turned and left him behind, heading for the driver's side door of my car. Shame and anger and guilt built up inside my gut, making me feel nauseated, making my heart burn in loss and indignation. I knew better than to get involved with shifters, but I'd still let Bastian into my life and my home. I'd accepted his words as truth when I should have doubted him. The man was a shifter, just like Aaric and the rest of the animals in his pack. My instincts were all wrong where men were concerned, especially male wolf shifters. I had to remember that and work through my problems without Bastian's help.

"Calla?"

I closed my eyes for just a second as my name floated across the cold air. That was the voice of the man I knew, the voice of the Bastian who'd calmed me and brought me food. That deep, rumbly way he'd been speaking to Aaric wasn't something I was used to or something I liked, but it was something that showed me the two sides to the man. He was hiding a lot from me, and I couldn't trust someone like that, especially not around my daughter.

"Thanks for fixing this," I said, refusing to look his way.

"Calla, wait."

"I'm tired, Bastian. Maybe another time."

"*Cariño*," he said as his fingers wrapped around my arm. Terror and fury exploded within me, memories of another shifter on another day grabbing me the same way. As he pushed me to the ground and rolled me onto my stomach. As he clung to my hips with fingers that turned into claws.

"No." Panicking, I yanked away from him and swung my door open to put space between us. "No waiting, no trusting, no believing in promises and words you don't mean. I need to do what's best for my daughter, and that means getting away from shifters. Forever."

# ELEVEN



I DOVE INTO MY truck as soon as Calla tore out of the lot, ready to rip the interior apart in my rage. Of all the fucking luck… Of *course* she had to see Aaric and me together. And of course I had to mind my damned manners with the man so as not to set off a pack war before I knew the situation. If I wouldn't have been drugged half into oblivion, I'd have been able to sense her coming. Or maybe just know how many wolves the man hung out with so I could evaluate the risks better.

I was never taking The Draught again.

I yanked open my glove box and dug for the leftover vials as my phone began to ring. But Calla didn't have a phone, so it wasn't her. And Calla was the only person I wanted to talk to. Ignoring the sound, I grabbed all my vials of Draught and opened the door, smashing them against the concrete as my phone continued to ring. And ring. And ring some more. Finally, I punched the steering wheel and grabbed the thing from my pocket.

"What?" I roared into the speaker, starting the engine and throwing my truck in gear.

"Put the truck in park, Beast."

I growled at the calm way Phoenix spoke to me, as if I was a child throwing a tantrum.

"What the hell do you know about it, kid?"

"I know you're pissed as shit, you're revving that engine like a speed demon, and that you're about to make a huge mistake. And I know how important that mate bond is, so if you want to save your relationship, you'll put the goddamned truck in park and listen to me, old man."

I paused at the driveway, tapping my fingers as I waited for traffic to clear so I could turn onto the highway. "I have to talk to her."

"Not tonight. Amber says—"

"Again with Amber? She's not the all-knowing psychic she claims to be." I squealed the tires as I hit the gas, heading for Calla's building. "It's her fault I'm in this mess."

"No, it's your fault you're in this mess. All she did was point you toward your mate."

I grunted, ready to toss the phone out the window. "And how exactly is this my fault?"

"How hard have you been hitting The Draught, man?"

I nearly slammed on the brakes, not at all prepared to hear those words. "What?"

"You know what." Phoenix's voice was quiet but intense, his disapproval clear. "I know you, Beast. You can call Gates for help and ask for Shadow instead of me, but that won't help you hide. I still know what you're doing."

"Phoenix," I said as I pulled over, my chest a little tight. "I just needed to chain up my wolf instincts."

"In a strange city, with no backup and no Breed member around to help you should things go sideways. That doesn't sound like a man who's thinking clearly, now does it?" He huffed, the line filling with static for a moment. "We've been there, done that with this, man. The night those shifters almost killed me, you saved my ass by giving me my wolf. And the day Amber did kill me, you saved it again."

My eyes closed, memories of Phoenix lying prone on the forest floor, not breathing, making my stomach churn and my palms go sweaty.

"That could have been any number of things."

"That's bullshit and you know it," he hissed, his anger clear. "Time and again, situations have proven the need for backup nearby, but you go running across the country without telling us. With your phone turned off so we can't reach you. You left me to beg Amber to use her powers just to make sure you're alive."

I sighed, dropping my chin to my chest as I fought off the wave of guilt. "I'm sor—"

"Fuck the apologies, man. Just listen to me this time. Stop The Draught, get your ass back to your hotel, and let this shit settle for the night."

"What if the guy comes back for her?"

"Amber says the pack is tailing your ass, not hers. Besides, Shadow's already there. He's at her building and will keep guard for you."

I swallowed, my arguments evaporating the more Phoenix spoke. "She's scared of shifters."

"And she's going to be completely terrified if you go over there right now with your temper blazing." There was mumbling in the background before Phoenix came back on the line. "Look, man, I know you're pissed at Amber, but she's trying to help you. And right now she's saying that if you show up at Calla's today, you'll lose her."

"Phoenix—"

"I know. I do," he said, his voice calm but firm. "But you gotta hold tight for one night, my brother. Just one. Everything will be okay if you can be patient."

"Patience isn't exactly my preferred virtue, man."

Phoenix chuckled. "Trust me, we all know that. But you need to be still for the night. Hunker down at your hotel and wait it out. While you're there, throw that Draught shit out and get some sleep. You're probably running on empty."

I rubbed a hand over my face, still not ready to leave my mate in someone else's hands. "I could just—"

There was what sounded like a scuffle, and then Amber's voice came over the line, sounding frantic. "If you try to guard her, you'll lose. If you go to her apartment, you'll lose. If you leave your hotel room tonight, you'll lose. And you have no idea how much hinges on this decision—more than just your relationship with the pregnant blonde. Stay in your hotel room tonight, Beast. I'm begging you."

I banged my head back against the headrest a few times, growling and feeling as if something was tearing my heart in two. "Fucking fine, okay? I'll stay inside."

Amber sighed. "Thank you, Beast. And don't worry. Shadow has your mate in his sights. He won't let anything happen to her."

I nodded even though she couldn't see me and flicked on my blinker to make a U-turn. "I'm giving you twelve hours, Polaroid. And then I'm on her doorstep, begging her to forgive me."

"Ten."

"What?"

"You'll be on her doorstep in ten hours; otherwise, you'll miss your chance. And you'll be brave and honest with her. Trust me."

# TWELVE

*Calla*

THE MORNING AFTER LEAVING Bastian standing in the parking lot behind the diner, I lay sprawled across my couch, berating myself in my mind. I was an idiot. I'd fallen into the same trap, believed the same lines from another man. *Sure*, Bastian wanted to help me. *Sure*, he'd be there for me. *Sure*, I could trust him.

I couldn't trust anyone—especially not another wolf shifter.

A knock at my door set my heart racing in my chest. I knew it was him even before I pulled myself up. What was he doing here? And what should I say? Did I let him in? Tell him to leave and never come back? My heart didn't want me to, but I couldn't listen to it. I needed to do what was right, which meant not allowing him into my life.

But when I opened the door and met those stunning blue eyes, I knew exactly how hard it was going to be to get rid of him.

"We need to talk," Bastian said while shifting around the bags he held.

I crossed my arms over my chest, trying to look tougher than I felt. "Go ahead, talk,"

He gave me a small, frustrated sigh before leaning into my space, hovering over my body. So close…so warm. And Jesus, he smelled good.

"I'm not going to freeze you by making you keep this door open," he said, his voice low and sensually gritty. "Please, may I come in? I promise to leave as soon as I tell you what you need to hear."

I glared at him for a moment, completely unsure of what to do next. My heart was calling for him, screaming at me to let him in. To listen to him. Trust his words. But my mind… Oh, my mind was on a totally different planet. My mind was telling me to slam the door in Bastian's face and never open it for him again.

It was his softly whispered, "Please, Calla," that did me in. My heart won…at least on the letting him in issue.

"You've got five minutes, tops."

"Understood." He set the bags on the counter and took off his coat. Feral Breed was loud and clear to me as I watched him, the growling wolf on the back indicating something completely different than it had before yesterday. This man was dangerous, and I needed to remember that.

"I want your full attention for a few minutes," he said, his eyes finding mine. "I'm going to say things that are hard for me. I don't normally…like to talk about this stuff. But someone told me to be brave and honest, so I'm going to be. For you. I'd like to make sure you hear me."

"Fine." I headed to the couch, wringing my hands and trying to clear my head. Bastian left me feeling so unsettled. So confused. Wanting so much to trust him at his word, but unable to.

Bastian followed me across the room, sitting on the coffee table and leaning into me as I curled up on the couch. He reached forward and grabbed my hands, his skin worn and tough against mine. And surprisingly, he looked me right in the eye.

"You're going to have a hard time believing this, but I want you to know. I need you to know the truth. What Aaric said about your being his mate was a lie. A flat-out lie. He can't track you by anything more than smell, and he can't sense you wherever you go. He's not your mate. There's no possible way."

"How do you know?"

He kept his eyes on mine even as I saw him swallow hard. Fearful.

"Because you're *my* mate," he said, his voice solid.

I couldn't speak, couldn't move, too stunned to even breathe.

"I know, I know," Bastian said, pulling me closer. "Aaric told you the same thing. But listen to me, wolf shifters usually only get one mate. One person—shifter or human—who the fates decreed was their perfect match. The attraction is instant. The feelings strong enough to last a lifetime. I ended up here because a witch showed me you. I didn't even realize I was running to you. I thought, because of the baby, that you were claimed by another and I couldn't have you, so I was running away from the pain that caused. But instead, I ended up here. I ended up in your diner. And that night, when you smiled at me for the first time, was the happiest I've ever been in my life."

"But—"

"No, Calla. No buts." Bastian got down on his knees in front of me. "You're my mate, and I've come for you. I know this is hard to believe, especially since Aaric lied to you before. But I swear on every life, every bible, every deity imaginable, I'm telling you the truth."

My heart lurched, the seriousness of his gaze and the intensity of his words speaking to me in more ways than any other language could. And yet, I couldn't fall again. Couldn't believe him. Not yet. Not without knowing.

"Are you in his pack?"

Bastian shook his head. "No, I haven't been in a pack since I was young. And I'd never met Aaric before yesterday. I swear."

"But he called you Beast instead of Bastian."

"It's a road name. My real name is Bastian, but my Feral Breed brothers call me Beast. I'm kind of…well-known in the shifter world."

I sat back, wrapping my arms around my knees. "You kill people."

His eye twitched, and he took a deep breath as he nodded. "I kill people who need to be killed. Usually wolf shifters who've turned bad and are murdering humans. Shifters who threaten to expose our world to yours. We can't have that, Calla. We rely on our secret to stay alive as a species. My club, the Feral Breed, we're like the National Guard of the wolf shifter world. We get called in when the pack rules aren't enough to keep a wolf in line. And if needed, we end the shifter who's out of control. But it's never without reason, and it's never an easy thing for any of us to do."

I sighed and shook my head as warring desires nearly tore my heart in two. "I don't know what to think."

"Think of me," Bastian said, crawling closer. "What do you feel when you're near me?"

"I don't know," I lied.

"Fine, I'll go first." Bastian gripped my hands tighter, inching closer. "I'm happy around you. Comforted for the first time in my very long life. I feel the need to stay next to you, to never leave your side. My heart calls for you, my body craves you, and I would do anything to keep you safe. You and your daughter. You became my family the day we met; I just haven't been man enough to tell you until now."

My heart raced, my mind spinning. This man. There was such honesty in his words. Such kindness. I hated not to trust him, but it was hard for me to accept him at face value. He was still a wolf shifter, just like Aaric—just like his pack—and I'd been fooled before.

"Bastian, I can't—"

"Just tell me this." He leaned over me, his face close enough for me to rub my nose against his. "Tell me the truth. Do you feel the attraction between us? Because if you do, if you can feel our bond, then you know. Deep down, you know I'm telling you the truth. If you can't"—he closed his eyes and licked his bottom lip—"I'll get you away from here, so you and your daughter can be safe, and then I'll leave you alone. I promise you, Calla. Just tell me the truth. Can you feel the connection between us? The desire to be close to me?"

For long seconds, I refused to answer. Refused to admit the intensity of my attraction to him. Because it scared me— the need I had to be close. To sit by him, stand next to him, just to be near him. I'd never experienced it before, never met someone I felt so attached to in such a short period of time. Scared me? Heck, it terrified me.

Finally, unable to lie to him again, holding his gaze the entire time, I nodded a subtle and shallow yes.

Bastian let out a rushed breath and pressed his forehead against mine. "Thank you, Calla. Thank you for being honest with me." He leaned back, his eyes bright, a smile on his face as he said, "That's our bond you feel. That's our link as mates."

"I don't know, Bastian."

"I'm not saying it has to be easy or perfect right from the start. I'm just asking for a chance. A shot to prove myself to you." He came closer, surrounding me with his warmth. "I'll earn your trust, Calla. I promise. I'll work my ass off for it."

I rested my hand against his cheek with a whispered, "Bastian." He made it so hard to think sometimes. His nearness, the size of him, the way he overpowered me with nothing but his presence. I shook my head, breaking our stare and wishing for time to process. Luckily for me, the baby answered my need.

"I have to get up," I whispered.

Bastian's face fell, and he sat back on his heels with his shoulders slumped in defeat.

"Yeah," he said, quietly. "Okay. I'll just go—"

"No." My answer came out fast, surprising me almost as much as it surprised Bastian. His head jerked up, his eyes meeting mine. "Don't go. I just…I have to…"

When Bastian cocked his head, I sighed. "The baby's kicking my bladder."

"Oh," Bastian said as he jumped to his feet. He grabbed my elbows and helped me off the couch, steadying me once I was standing in front of him. "Do you need any help?"

I raised my eyebrows at him. "Pretty sure I can handle it."

He choked on a laugh, shaking his head. "Yeah, sorry. That came out wrong."

I trailed my hand down his arm as I waddled toward the hall, even that minor separation making my chest tighter. When I reached the door to the bathroom, I turned, catching Bastian staring after me.

"You'll still be here, right? I mean, you're not…"

He shook his head as a slow smile crept up his face. "I'm not going anywhere unless you tell me to, *cariño*."

I nodded and walked into the bathroom, but then I darted back out. "Hey, Bastian?"

He was in front of me before I finished saying his name, his eyes filled with concern. "Yes?"

"What's that mean?"

"What…*cariño*?" Bastian smiled and brought a hand to my cheek, running his finger down to my jaw as he whispered, "It means sweetheart. My father called my mother *cariño* from the day they met."

"Oh," I said, my heart melting inside of me. "Okay, thanks."

"My pleasure." He turned to walk back into the living room. My eyes wandered down to the seat of his jeans, watching the muscles bunch and lengthen with every step. But then I sighed, quelling the arousal building within with a quick shake of my head. It was time for me to think, not fantasize about Bastian touching me more. Touching me in other places. Those rough hands rubbing all over my body.

"Calla? You okay?"

I jumped, my face burning as Bastian's voice pulled me from my naughty daydreams. "Yeah, I'm fine. I'll be right out."

And with that, I escaped into the bathroom, trying hard to ignore the throaty chuckle I heard from Bastian.

# THIRTEEN



I WAITED ON TENTERHOOKS for Calla to come back. This had to work. I'd spent the whole night pacing in my hotel room, practically ready to claw through the walls to get to my mate. My instincts had been screaming that only I could keep her safe, but Phoenix's calm voice had played through my head, reminding me of my goal. I had to wait; I had to stay away to keep her safe. So wait I did. I waited the longest ten hours of my life.

My wolf spirit was slowly coming back up through the haze The Draught had forced him into, my senses sharpening with every hour. My instincts slowly coming back to life. I'd scented Shadow on my way inside but couldn't pinpoint where he was hiding. I could tell that a female shifter had been inside Calla's apartment at some point, but I couldn't determine how long ago that visit had been. And I finally figured out why Calla always smelled a bit like wolf. The slow response and filtered senses left me feeling a bit off-balance, so I was thankful Shadow was still outside, guarding Calla and me, just in case.

After several minutes, Calla appeared, looking wary but not scared. No, there was no fear in her. Just an apprehensive questioning vibe that made something warm and filled with possibility bloom inside of me. Something that felt a bit like hope.

She watched me for a long, tense moment, standing as still as stone at the entry to her hall.

"Tell me about mating."

I nodded, psyching myself up internally for this conversation. Moving across the room, we came together to sit on opposite ends of the couch, the divide between us wide but not hostile.

I rubbed a hand over my chin, the scruff of having not shaved that morning raspy under my skin. "What do you want to know?"

"How do you know I'm your mate?" she asked, her face serious, betraying nothing. "You said you saw me."

I nodded. "One of my denmates, a man by the name of Phoenix, is mated to a witch. Her sister did a spell thing to give me sight of my mate, not by my choice, though. She said she'd been getting flashes of you and was concerned that you needed me." I held my hands up as she sat up straighter, a glare in her eyes. "Hey, you've been doing great on your own. She meant you were in danger, which was the only reason I let her show me. So that I could figure out what to do to help you."

She sat back, calmer again. "But you ran away instead of coming here."

"I did. I thought the baby meant you were married. I'm not the most honorable man, but I would never come between someone's vows that way. I promised I would stay away, maybe check in now and again to make sure you were safe and comfortable." I dropped my head and swallowed hard, voicing words that I had never wanted to admit. "But I was very disappointed that I couldn't claim my mate. I've walked the earth a long time by myself."

Calla shifted, inching closer. "How old are you?"

"Two hundred and nine."

Her eyes went wide "Seriously?"

"Yeah." I shrugged.

"That's really…sad."

I felt my eyebrow furrow at her question. "What is?"

"You finally find your mate, and I'm human. You'll only get to have me for my human lifespan." She looked away, her cheeks darkening.

My heart soared. Her eyes were unfocused across the room, but her admission told me she was thinking about me as a possibility. A potential suitor in her life.

I moved closer, our knees touching. "If you were to agree to be my mate, I would give you a claiming bite. It would slow your aging."

Her eyes returned to mine, questioning. "How slow?"

I shrugged. "I know of human men and women who have lived for centuries by the side of their mate."

She sat quiet for a moment, letting her mind turn over my words. I knew where her thoughts had gone when she opened her eyes wide, her hands sliding over her stomach protectively.

"My daughter."

I leaned forward, placing my hand over hers. "You won't have to say goodbye to her. This little one is a shifter."

She glanced to where my hand covered hers. "How do you know?"

"I can smell it. You smell wolflike, though not as if you were claimed or had been scented by a lover. It confused me at first."

"What do you mean, you can smell it?"

"We have enhanced senses. Smell, sight, taste, hearing. Like right now, I can tell that there's been a female shifter in your apartment, though not when she was here the last time."

"Two weeks ago," she whispered. "I can't go to the regular doctor, so Aaric has a woman from his pack come examine me."

"That would explain it."

Calla's breathing had picked up, her face flushed. I hadn't noticed how close we were sitting until that moment, when I looked into her eyes and realized our lips were about an inch apart. Our breaths mingling.

"What was that other thing?" she asked, her voice rough.

"What other thing? The being scented by a lover comment?"

"Yes," she whispered. "What does that mean?"

"It's kind of hard to explain." I leaned forward, practically crowding her back in the corner. "Can I show you?"

She nodded, her eyes still on mine, her lip pulled between her teeth. Damn, I wanted to bite that pink bit of flesh, replace her teeth with mine. Taste her mouth as I covered her body with my own.

Instead of kissing her, I lowered my head, placing my cheek against hers. I rubbed against her, sniffing, embedding her scent in my brain and mine on her skin. When she giggled, I pulled away.

"Sorry," I said, my lips so close to hers I couldn't help but stare.

"It's fine," she replied, her hands coming up to grip my arms. "I like the way it tickles."

I hummed and went back to rubbing my nose up and down her neck, moving slowly until I lay beside her on the couch. My lips moved against her skin, not kissing, just sliding over. Not tasting yet, just…enhancing the scenting of her as mine.

She shivered under my touch, and her breathing sped up. When she moved, edging against me and pressing her hip into my dick, the scent of her arousal had me granite hard in a matter of seconds.

"Bastian," she moaned. I pulled her closer, wrapping my arms around her, caging her in as I ran my nose along her jawline.

"Yes, Calla?"

She leaned up, just enough to bring her lips to mine. A soft tickle of flesh that made my heart race and my cock twitch. Right there. She was right there. Waiting for me to kiss her, to take what I wanted. And I would have; I would have taken her lips with mine and owned them. If I'd had a chance.

But instead, she kissed me.

My brave, independent mate pressed her lips to mine, brought her hands up to grip my face, and pulled me almost on top of her. I groaned and dove into the kiss, sliding my tongue past her parted lips to taste that sweet mouth. She met me stroke for stroke, her passion obvious. Her body responding with every breath.

I gripped her hip, twisting to keep my weight off the baby. But Calla wasn't happy with that, with the space I'd put between us. She yanked me closer, her kiss turning more aggressive. I followed her lead, curling over and around her, letting my hands wander tentatively along her body.

"Bastian," she gasped, throwing her head back as I nibbled her neck.

"Yes, *cariño*?"

"This doesn't mean I believe you."

I smiled and moved my lips back to hers, kissing her again.

"That's okay. I'll just tell you again tomorrow." Kiss. "And the next day." Kiss. "And the day after that."

I pulled back to capture her gaze, letting myself be as open and honest as I could. "I will be here every day to tell you how much you mean to me, how much I want to take care of you, and how much I desire your presence in my life." I put my hand on her belly, making sure she understood. "Both of you."

Her eyes went soft, tears forming. "Please don't lie to me."

"I swear." I kissed her again, this time down her neck to the swell of her breasts before looking up to once again meet her gaze. "On my name, on my honor, on my life. You're my mate, and I'll always be here to remind you of what that means to me."

She held my gaze, her hand joining mine on her stomach as I inched my way up her body. The moment felt heavy with meaning, filled with a sense of acceptance and trust. Calla moved first again, kissing me softly, sweetly. But then she groaned, and I gave up all sense of soft and sweet. Our lips crashed together, tongues tangling, hands grasping. Fighting to be closer, but unable to move how we needed due to our position. She yanked on my shoulder, trying to pull me on top of her, but there was no way for me to do that safely.

I shook my head. "I don't want to hurt you or the baby."

"I know. I'm just…I'm so…" She groaned, the sound going straight to my cock.

"What do you want, Calla?" I slid my hands up her stomach to just below her breasts. "Tell me, and I'll give it to you. Anything you need."

She groaned again, dropping her head back as I moved my hand up to palm her heavy breast. She may not be able to say the words, but her body was telling me everything I needed to know. Her breathing was fast, her cheeks flushed. Her nipples stood proud underneath the oversized T-shirt she wore and her hips were shifting every few minutes, as if searching for a comfortable position or a little stimulation. I had no doubt that my mate was in need of release.

"You seem so tense, my sweet." I leaned down to whisper in her ear. "Can I help you? Will you let me give you what you need?"

She groaned as my fingers tweaked her nipple, her entire body responding to the stimulation.

"Oh, my. You *are* in need, aren't you? Can I help you? I promise to make you feel good." I slid my hand over her belly, stopping when I reached the waistband to her stretchy pants. "Just tell me yes, Calla."

"Bastian." Calla dropped her hand to mine, sliding our joined fingers into her pants.

I kissed her nose and moved a bit lower on the couch, angling my hand to go deeper, reach what we both wanted me to reach. "I've got you, *cariño*. Just trust me."

Down through the patch of tight curls and over her pelvic bone I went, slowly working my way to her pussy. Giving her the chance to tell me no. Finally, my fingers met swollen, wet flesh, my touch causing Calla to shiver. I groaned, wishing for a taste of her, but knowing she wasn't ready for that yet.

The moment I slipped a finger over her clit, she gasped and nearly jumped off the couch, her body strung tight. I grunted and held her in place, adding more pressure as I whispered in her ear.

"So soft and wet. You've been needy for a while, haven't you? My poor girl." I spread my fingers on either side of her clit, moving my hand back and forth in slow strokes. "I'll never leave you wanting. I'll make sure you get what you need."

She twitched and shivered as I teased her, breathy little squeaks coming every few strokes. Once I had her on edge—her back straining and her eyes clenched shut—I shifted my hand farther down. Sliding two fingers inside her, I pressed the heel of my palm against her swollen clit and used my entire hand to grip and tease.

"Yes," she groaned, biting her lip as her knees lifted and spread.

"That's it, *cariño*. Feel me. You're so close. I want to feel you come around my fingers. I want you to suck me in."

"Bas—" she gasped as her back arched, riding the edge of her pleasure. One final push from me and she came with a groan, her walls spasming around my fingers as her body trembled.

"Good girl." I kept my palm against her clit, pulling her through the orgasm. "There you go, my sweet. That's it. Let me make it good for you."

"Oh God." Calla grabbed my head and yanked me down

for a deep kiss as her entire body tensed one final time. I eased up on the pressure of my hand but left my fingers just inside her, sliding along the edge of her lips. My wolf spirit howled a happy song, the way our mate responded to us waking him more than anything else I'd tried.

Finally, Calla relaxed against the couch and opened her eyes, staring into mine. Cheeks flushed and pupils wide, she looked like a happy woman. A sated one. And that was something that made me want to puff my chest up in pride.

"I can't," she whispered, shaking her head as she watched me. "I don't…"

As Calla stumbled over her words, I smiled and leaned over to kiss her into silence.

"Next time, it'll be my tongue you come around."

"Next time?" Her eyes stared into mine, a shadow of that mistrust lingering in their depths. I hated that expression. Hated knowing how badly someone else had screwed up to make her look at me like that.

"Give me a chance to hold you up, Calla. I promise I won't let you fall," I murmured, kissing her chin, her cheek, and up to her ear. "Don't compare me to Aaric."

She peered up at me as I moved back, her eyes wide. "I'm trying."

"And I appreciate it." I grinned, unable to hold back the happiness being so close to her had made me feel. I pulled my hand from her pants, giving her clit one last swipe along the way, loving how that tiny touch made her hips jump. "Why don't we get cleaned up? I have to check in with my Breed denmates real quick to make sure they're all here."

"Here? As in, in town?"

I nodded. "We're going to get you out of here, you and your baby. I called in a couple of people to help me, just in case."

Calla grew quiet, her eyes watching me warily all of a sudden. "Do they know?"

"Know what?"

She looked away, suddenly shy. "About me? Do they know you found your mate?"

"Of course. I told them when I called for their help. I would have shouted it from the rooftops if I could have, but your safety is my first priority, which means Aaric and his pack wolves can't find out." I took a deep breath and leaned my forehead on her shoulder. "I've been suppressing my wolf instincts so as not to scare you, but I have to let them out now. I need every advantage in case Aaric or one of his men comes around."

"And your friends are willing to help me?"

"Absolutely. You say the word, and we'll go. But Calla"—I met her eyes with mine, making sure she heard me—"you need to decide soon. Because if Aaric comes near you again, or if I think you're in any kind of danger, we're going whether you're ready or not. I won't let him hurt you."

Her eyes filled with tears, her breath catching. "I prayed for you," she whispered. "I couldn't get out by myself so I prayed for someone to come and help me. And you showed up."

"I'll always come for you. No matter what." I pressed my lips to hers as her tears fell, wishing I could quell her fears.

"Thank you, Bastian," she whispered.

I shook my head. "You're my mate; there's no need to thank me. I'd walk through fire for you." My stomach sank as my statement pulled a harsh memory, those words truer than I'd ever understood. I kissed her head and pulled myself up from the couch. "I just need to run outside and talk to the guy guarding your apartment, and then I'll be back."

Calla looked surprised. "There's someone guarding my apartment?"

"Of course. He's been there since yesterday. I knew you needed a little time to yourself after last night, but I couldn't leave you alone." I shrugged. "I won't risk you or the baby."

My mate rolled to the edge of the couch and pushed herself up to sitting. I stood and helped her to her feet, unsure of her intentions. Until she grabbed my shirt and yanked me down to her level.

"You are a very sweet man."

I grinned. "Pretty sure you're the only person who's ever said that."

"Good." She rose up on the balls of her feet to plant a deep, wet kiss on my lips, leaving me nearly breathless. "Hurry back?"

"Yeah," I breathed, bringing a hand to my mouth to savor the tingle her kiss gave me. She smirked and headed for the bathroom as I rushed to throw my coat on. As soon as the bathroom door closed, I sprinted out the door and down the stairs, heading for the relative privacy of my truck. Luckily, I didn't cross paths with Shadow, but I knew he was around. Hopefully, he'd make himself scarce for a few minutes.

As soon as I hopped inside my truck, I yanked open the fly of my jeans. Fuck, I was hard. So desperately needing to come. My hand still smelled of her, the scent of her arousal teasing me and driving me mad with lust. Remembering the way she said my name as she came, I wrapped my fingers around my cock, stroking strong and hard.

"Jesus, Calla." I thrust into my hand, gripping my cock hard and rubbing over the tip on each stroke. It felt so good, giving in to my needs with my mate's scent all around me. I pulled on my frenum, wondering how Calla would react to it. How it would feel with her pulling on the steel, licking it… sliding it inside her.

An embarrassingly low number of strokes were all it took for me to come all over my hand. Sitting back, breathing hard, I looked down at myself and smiled. My mate had gotten me to this point. Someday, if I was very careful and extremely lucky, it would be her hand wrapped around me as I came. Her mouth. Her pussy. Jesus, just the thought of sliding into that wet heat made me want to go again.

Instead, I reached into the glove box for my handy wipes and tucked myself back into my jeans. After cleaning myself up and taking a few minutes to calm my raging heart, I stepped out of the truck and went to find Shadow. Not that I needed to look too hard, the man in question was leaning against the stairwell leading up to Calla's apartment.

"What's up, man?" I asked as I approached. Shadow and I had never been particularly close, but he was a sneaky son of a bitch. And fast. Shadow could get in and get out of just about any place without being detected. I'd asked Gates to bring him in case Aaric was able to get past me and take Calla to the pack grounds. A man like Shadow would be invaluable in a reverse kidnapping. Plus he was an old Army medic; those skills could come in handy.

"Beast." Shadow nodded, never one to mince words. "Got a plan for me?"

I huffed and glanced up the stairs. "Call Gates. I want everything in place before this asshole decides to act. I've got a bad feeling he's just waiting for the opportunity."

Shadow nodded and pulled a phone from his pocket. "On it. He and Kaija should be rolling into town in a few hours. They got held up in Chicago."

"What for?"

"Kaija and Blaze's mate Moira were going over another Omega kidnapping. Fuckers took a pup."

"How young?"

"Fifteen."

I whistled. "We need to catch these bastards."

"Agreed. But first"—he pointed up the stairs—"go nap. You look like shit. I'll guard."

"Thanks, man." I hurried up the stairs, anxious to get back. "Stay warm."

Shadow snorted. "Not fucking possible."

Back in the apartment, I closed and locked the door. Calla had turned the lights off in the living room, the only glow coming from the hallway. Her bedroom to be exact.

"Bastian?"

"Yeah, Calla. It's just me." I stripped out of my coat and took off my boots. When I stood back up, Calla was in the doorway to her room. Wearing flannel pants and a sweatshirt, she looked suddenly small and fragile as the light shone through her hair.

"I know I let you do…stuff, and I'm not saying we'll never…but I don't want to be alone…and I'm really tired—"

I smiled. "*Cariño?*"

She paused, peering at me. "Yeah?"

"I'd really like to just lie together and hold you for a bit. Would that be okay?"

She sighed and smiled. "You read my mind."

I laughed as I walked down the hall, pulling my shirt off as I went. "Not at all, I just happen to know a woman with doubts when I see one."

I walked right into her, pressing her up against the wall with my chest as she stared at me. I waited and watched, almost feeling her eyes as they traveled over ink and muscle, taking me in. She raised an eyebrow when she noticed the barbell through my left nipple.

"Pierced?"

I nodded. "And that's not the only one."

Her eyes went wide and her jaw fell open. I laughed and pulled her into my arms, leaning down to kiss those plump lips.

"C'mon, let's take a nap. I want to snuggle with you."

"You want to snuggle?" she asked, giving me a disbelieving look as I dragged her toward her bed.

"Yeah." I sat on the edge and pulled her between my spread legs, running my hands up and down the sides of her belly and pressing my lips to the crown. "Now listen here, little miss.

Your momma needs some rest, so settle down and give her a few hours of peace. If you do, I promise to get you—" I glanced up at Calla and raised my eyebrow.

"Milk."

Smiling, I whispered, "Milk. I'll make sure you get lots of cold milk. So go to sleep"—I closed my eyes as my mother's words came back to me—"before the faeries come."

I kissed Calla's belly, listening to the sound of the baby's heartbeat for just a moment. Soft, barely discernable even with my wolf senses coming back. A beautiful reminder of what possibilities life held for me. I just needed to convince Calla to trust me. "Rest, little angel."

Calla smiled and pushed me back, crawling onto the bed beside me. We shuffled and rolled until we found a comfortable position—her on her side with my thigh between her knees.

As she closed her eyes and laid her forehead against my chest, I truly understood the bliss that a mate could bring. And the terror her being in danger could instill.

# FOURTEEN



I HEADED DOWN THE stairs, bracing against the wind. I would have run to my car earlier to make sure it started if Bastian hadn't been there. I grinned, unable to stop… Bastian had stayed the afternoon with me. Napping in my bed. Curled around me. It was honestly the best sleep I'd gotten in months. The man was a walking furnace; plus, the way he surrounded me, practically lying across me, made me feel watched over. I wanted him in my bed all the time.

Bastian stood leaning against the side of his running truck, waiting for me. His leather-clad arms crossed over his chest. Black knit cap pulled down low on his forehead. Crooked smile on his handsome face. The man was just so…masculine. A real man. All grit and muscle, with a confidence that made my knees weak.

I slowed my approach, a smile spreading across my face as he watched me. Inspected me.

"Hi." I stopped in front of him, my belly nearly touching him. He dropped his arms to his sides, his fingers brushing my hips.

"Hello." His smile grew as he stared at my lips with a

hunger in his eyes. I wanted to jump into his arms and kiss the smile right off his face, but I couldn't risk it. Not yet, not with the possibility of Aaric or one of his packmates lurking nearby.

"You ready to go?" he asked. My stomach lurched. Was I? I knew he was asking if I was ready to go to work, but the there was a duality to the question. Was I ready to leave this town? To trust him enough to go with him?

I nodded even as my mind spun, walking beside him toward the passenger side of the truck. "So, I was thinking."

"About what?" he asked as he reached for the door handle. I grabbed his elbow, stopping him.

"Where's your friend?" I asked. "The one watching my apartment."

Bastian's eyebrow came down, his face questioning. "He's around back. Why?"

"Maybe I should meet him." I shrugged, playing casual even though my heart was racing at the thought of what I was about to do. "I figure I should know who he is in case I'm alone and see him. A shifter hanging around the halls…"

A shiver not caused by the cold blasted through me. Aaric and his packmates had taught me to fear shifters. But Bastian was kind, a noble prince buried beneath armor of ink and gruffness. Maybe if I met his teammate, I'd be more comfortable with the idea of wolf shifters running around outside my building.

Bastian leaned into the side of the truck, watching me closely. "Are you sure? You don't have to meet them now."

My heart stuttered. "Them?"

Bastian nodded. "My brother and his mate arrived while we were sleeping. All three are here."

"Your brother," I whispered, fear making my voice weak. "The Gate guy."

"The Gatekeeper, yes." Bastian watched me for a moment, weighing something he saw on my face. "We can do this another time if you're scared. Maybe go somewhere public and…normal. Like a store."

"No," I said quickly, pushing past the fear squeezing my chest. "I want to meet them, I do. I'm just…you know how…I don't want—"

"Calla?"

"Yeah?"

"I know shifters make you nervous," he said, leaning over me and holding my gaze. "I'd never introduce you to one I thought would hurt you. These are my denmates and my family. I trust them. Besides, you're safe with me."

I nodded and took a deep breath. "I know."

"No, you don't. But you'll see. You'll always be safe with me." He took a step back and whistled loud and long. Keeping his eyes on mine, he waited, his presence staying the panic I felt bubbling up from within. But then he turned, his head whipping to the left. I followed the path of his eyes, reaching for his arm and clutching on to him for dear life.

Two men and a woman walked out from around the side of the building, all graceful but almost unnaturally cautious in their movements. Animals unsure of their surroundings, wary of possible danger.

The woman didn't scare me as much as I would have expected. Short, with long blond hair and a huge smile, she appeared sweet and friendly. But the men. One looked a lot like my Bastian, sans scars, which meant he must have been the brother. There was something in the intensity of his gaze, the air of aggression about him, that made me want to hide behind Bastian. This man was a warrior, someone who battled and won. He was also calculating. The way his eyes bored into me told me he wasn't just looking at me; he was absorbing everything about me to find my weaknesses. To find a way through me.

But it was the third shifter—the other male—who immediately made me want to run. Taller and more lithe than Bastian, but somehow more of a predator than the others, he stalked as if the world were filled with his prey. Watched me with the eyes of an animal. He stopped twenty feet away or so, but the other two moved closer, not pausing until they stood beside us.

"Calla," Bastian said, smiling. "This is my brother, Lorenzo, though my denmates know him as Gates. And this is his mate, Kaija, otherwise known as Princess."

"Hello, Calla," Lorenzo said. "It's very nice to meet you." Like Bastian, Lorenzo's eyes brightened when he smiled, little lines forming at the corners as his cheeks lifted. He nodded to me and then looked down to his wife…mate…as she elbowed him in the ribs.

"Quit hogging her." The woman, Kaija, stepped closer, grabbing both my hands before I could stop her. Her eyes were also blue, but a deeper color than the brothers'. More ocean than sky.

"It's so good to finally meet you," Kaija said with a grin. She bent down, her nearly white hair sliding over her shoulder as she spoke to my belly. "And you, little one. We're going to have so much fun once you arrive." Standing up, her pale skin flushed a bit as she shrugged. "I miss my nephews, and I've never had a niece. I'm really excited to be her auntie."

"Jesus, Kai." Bastian sighed.

"What?" The woman looked up at him, all brave and confident even in the face of someone so much bigger than she. "Calla's your mate, and that baby comes along with the package. We might as well set up pack dynamic early."

Lorenzo moved to Bastian's side and threw an arm over his shoulders. "Give it up, man. There's no stopping her once she gets an idea in her head."

"Men." Kaija gave her mate a mock glare before smiling at me once more. "C'mere, sister. Let's give these boys a minute to talk about world domination."

"Oh," I said when she pulled me away from the truck.

I glanced over my shoulder at Bastian, who looked a little concerned.

"Don't worry," Kaija said. "First, I'd never hurt you. You're Bastian's mate, which means we're family. And I'd fight to the death for my family." She glanced at me, the animal side of her making itself known in the fierceness of her gaze. But then her smile returned. "And second, there's no way he'll let you out of his sight or his hearing range." When my eyes widened, she shrugged. "Privacy in a pack of shifters is just an illusion."

"Really?"

She nodded. "Yep. Like I could smell Bastian on you as soon as we turned the corner of the building. Your scents are interwoven now, but not completely, which means he scented you but you haven't had sex."

"Oh." My face heated as she giggled.

"Don't be shy. As a culture, we're much more open about sex than your people are. It's natural, it's fun, it feels good—"

"It gets you into trouble." I rested my hand on my swollen belly as we reached the stairs leading up to my apartment level, the building keeping the wind at bay. Kaija's smile turned sweet and her voice lowered.

"Children are a blessing. Especially little shifter girls, who are so rare in our world."

"Really?"

"Oh yes, only maybe one out of ten shifters born are females. If that. Add to that the fact that she'll be born during our breeding season, which is when most shifter babies are conceived. Only shifters mated to human females have babies outside of the late fall birthing season. And to be carrying an Omega shifter at that. You're very lucky."

"Omega?"

She cocked her head, a very animalistic move. "You didn't know?"

"I don't even know what that means."

"Well, Omegas, like me, are the rarest of all shifters. We carry an innate power to strengthen our pack. Omegas are always female, and until I met you and felt the Omega connection to my little niece here, I'd thought we were always born from the union of two shifters." She reached for my belly, pausing with her hand mere inches away until I nodded my permission. I barely felt her hand through the thickness of my coat, her touch light and kind.

"You must be one heck of a strong woman to carry an Omega, Calla. This little one is a blessing in so many ways, to you and to the rest of us. It's good your mate is as strong and caring as Bastian. He'll be a good father for her."

I stared at her as she smiled with a knowing expression on her face. As if the future was a done deal and she was just waiting for it to happen. I envied her confidence, her surety that things would work out.

Putting a little bit of faith in this woman I'd just met, I whispered, "I don't know if I can trust him yet."

"Yes, you do. You're just putting up roadblocks because of what this Aaric did to you." Kaija leaned forward, voice soft but eyes intense. "You do know Aaric manipulated you, right?"

My stomach clenched, and I felt the burn of tears in my eyes as I said a quiet, "Yes."

Kaija huffed. "When I think of how sacred mating bonds are. And for him to lie about it! To endanger the secret of shifter existence, I just don't understand. Why would he do such a thing? It's a crime punishable by death. What could he possibly be trying to gain?"

"He said I was his."

Kaija's expression turned hard, her anger evident. "He lied."

"He said he could feel me wherever I went."

"He lied." She growled, eyes growing more lupine.

"He said we'd be together forever." I took a step away from her, readying myself for my final argument.

"He lie—"

"And Bastian tells me the same things."

Kaija froze, eyes wide as she stared at me, speechless. I could understand why. No matter how many times I ran it over in my head, the truth of the matter was that Bastian told me the same words Aaric had. And though I felt closer to Bastian, more comfortable, I'd only just met him. How could I fully trust him when the story sounded the same?

But then Kaija's face fell into a soft smile, a look of understanding there. "But you can trust Bastian. You already do. Otherwise you wouldn't be here."

I shook my head. "I don't know."

"Yes, you do. Get those mental roadblocks out of the way so you can follow your instincts." She waved a hand at the men, who were watching us from their place by the truck. "Wolves are all about their instincts, and you've got a little pup inside you with instincts to spare. She'll help you find the path. You just need to get out of your own way to reach it."

TEN MINUTES AND A quick goodbye later, we were in the truck and headed to the diner. My conversation with Kaija had left me feeling a bit off, as if there was something I needed to know, but it was just out of my reach.

Bastian wrapped his hand around mine after turning onto the highway.

"You okay?"

"Yeah," I said, my voice quiet. "Lorenzo and Kaija were very nice."

"They are," Bastian said with a nod. "So is Shadow, but you seemed really nervous, so he stayed back."

"I didn't mean to be rude," I said, even though I was glad the catlike man hadn't gotten too close.

"You weren't rude. All shifters understand the fight-or-fight instincts we sometimes bring out in humans. But I can tell you, he's a good man. Honest and trustworthy."

I hummed, staring out the window as my mind went in circles. "He reminds me of a cat."

"Huh?"

"The way he walks and his eyes." I turned to face him as he glanced my way. "He's more cat than wolf to me."

Bastian was silent for a moment, a frown on his face. "I guess I never noticed, but I can see your point. He's quiet and calm, and sneaky as all get-out."

I shrugged. "Like a cat."

I chewed my lip the rest of the way to the diner, lost in my own head as I thought about cats and dogs and claws. When we reached the lot, I didn't open the door right away. Instead, I sat and stared at Bastian, still trying to work out whatever had my thoughts all tied up in knots. Poor Bastian sat on edge, looking stiff, tense, and ready to defend himself.

"What if you're wrong?" I finally asked.

"Wrong about what?"

"About me. What if you're wrong and we're not mates?"

"Not possible," he said, strong and sure.

"How do you know?"

"Because there's no way not to." Bastian sighed and rubbed a hand over his hair. "I know because I feel it. The thread that the fates used to tie you to me is right here"—he placed a hand over his heart—"and I can feel it. Every day. Every second. You're right here, wrapped around my heart. How could I not know you're my fated match when my heart is so sure?"

I leaned forward and took his hand, placing it against my own heart. "I feel it too, but I'm scared."

"I know," he whispered. "You're my mate, my only one, and I'll keep telling you and showing you until you believe me. Believe us."

I swallowed, my heart racing under our joined hands. "I

think I'll get there."

"I know you will." Bastian's eyes turned dark, his breathing speeding up. "I want to kiss you so fucking bad right now, *cariño.*"

"I know," I said with a nod, telling him with my eyes how much I wanted to be kissed by him. We sat in a tense silence, knowing we couldn't have what we wanted. Not yet. Not where people could see.

Finally, Bastian sighed. "You have to get inside or you'll be late."

"Yeah."

"Get to work," he said as he squeezed my hand one more time before letting it go. "I'll be here when you're done. And then we can talk about getting you out of here. Because that needs to happen…soon."

I nodded, unable to speak. My head knew the conversation was needed, and my heart was ready for him. But something still held me back. Leaving with him wouldn't solve my problems, not really. Because if he ever left me, I'd be helpless again.

But this time, he'd take my heart with him.

# FIFTEEN



I CREPT FORWARD, MY claws extended into the snow for purchase. The pack camp sat in a shallow valley two hundred yards away. With my wolf senses, I could still hear and see what was happening. I wasn't close enough for them to smell me unless the wind shifted, which was a good thing as I'd been spying on them for the past few hours.

I'd spent the late afternoon and early evening hours running in wolf form, relying on my senses to clear my head of the aftereffects of The Draught. It'd worked well. Just a day off the stuff, and I was able to track Aaric through town and out to his camp. Fucker had no idea I was so close.

I hadn't seen anything too far out of the ordinary in the hours I'd been watching, though that didn't mean I wasn't still on edge. These shifters had threatened my mate. I wouldn't underestimate the danger they posed to her and her baby.

As I lay and watched, a car pulled into camp. Three men hopped out, two from the front and one from the back. They converged on the remaining rear door, opening it and grasping the arms of a stumbling red-haired female. She looked pale and sick from my vantage point, and the way they had to carry her into a cabin fit that theory. I wanted to move closer, see if I could determine her illness, but the wind felt far too unsteady. I was afraid it'd turn and expose me, so instead, I buried myself in the snow and waited.

When the sun barely touched the top of the trees to my west, quiet paw steps sounded through the darkening forest. I sniffed, ready for a fight, until the other wolf's scent washed over me. Gates, in his huge black wolf form so much like my own, padded up. Near-silent on his feet, he'd been able to get too close to me for comfort. A sure sign that my senses weren't all the way back from The Draught-induced sleep yet.

Gates lay down beside me, wiggling his own burrow in the snow as he watched the camp. There was no need to attempt communication. He knew what my fears would be in regards to my new mate, and he'd do anything to keep her safe for me. Just as I'd do anything for Kaija. Feral Breed notwithstanding, we were brothers. Family. And we'd almost lost each other after the death of our parents. If there was one thing our father had taught us both, it was to never make the same mistakes twice.

As the moon rose in the sky, I chuffed softly and rose to my feet. It was nearing time to pick up Calla. Gates followed me through the snow-covered woods as we snuck the six miles back to the road where I'd left my truck. Gates' truck was parked beside mine, a testament to the man's tracking ability.

"Seen anything?" Gates asked once in his human form. He slid hurriedly into his clothes, the cold night air making us both shiver.

"Red-haired shewolf arrived earlier. Looked ill."

"Bringing sickness into the pack? That doesn't sound right."

I shrugged. "Couldn't get closer because of the wind. I'll be keeping an eye on it, though. At least for as long as we're here."

Gates huffed, sniffing hard, learning more about the woods. "What's the plan for tonight?"

"Shadow and Kaija?"

"Shadow's guarding Calla at the diner, and Kaija's back at the hotel."

I nodded. "Let's meet her there. I can fill you two in before I have to pick Calla up from work."

"You chauffeuring her around?" He smirked as I glared his way. The jackass.

"Like you wouldn't do the same if you knew Kaija was in danger."

His smirk fell as a growl rumbled through his chest. "I'd do whatever it took to keep her safe."

"Exactly." I headed to my truck, glancing back when I reached the door. "Now imagine that times two."

Gates cocked his head. "Two?"

"Calla and the baby she's carrying. Two." I hopped inside with a grunt, staring at him through the open door. "No one's touching either of them."

"Daddy Beast." Gates gave me a small grin as he backed toward his truck. "I'm glad you called, brother. Let's find a way to keep your new family safe."

BACK AT THE HOTEL, I sat in Gates and Kaija's room, biting my thumbnail and bouncing my leg. Gates had called for Shadow to join us, leaving Calla unprotected. I wasn't happy about that, but I knew we needed a few minutes all together to get a plan in place. Still, my eyes kept darting to the window where I could see the diner sign down the road.

Shadow sprawled on the floor, exhausted but awake, his long legs trailing over the threshold and into the bathroom. My brother and Kaija sat on the edge of the bed, shoulders touching and hands joined. Waiting for me to start. Since this mission revolved around my mate, any plans would have to go through me. The risk was all mine.

"Here's what I know," I said as I leaned forward and placed

my elbows on my thighs. "Aaric meets Calla and tells her she's his mate. He also tells her about the blood-sensing mated couples can do once they exchange claiming marks. Calla gets pregnant; Aaric flips his switch."

"Flips how?" Kaija asks.

"He dropped the good-guy act, threatened her, roughed her up from what I can gather, and he made no effort to help her through the pregnancy though he wants this baby. He's told her he'll take it from her if he has to." A growl rumbled in my chest in response to hers. "He doesn't support her, and Calla lives in near-poverty. The first time I went over, there was practically no food, the place was cold, and she obviously didn't have much beyond the essentials."

"No self-respecting shifter would allow his mate and child to live that way," Gates said.

"She's not his mate." The words came out as a growl, my lip curling in response to the fury his words brought out of me. Coughing it back, I offered my brother a sheepish head nod as an apology, which he accepted with a lift of one side of his mouth. Fuck, he had to know how hard it was to hear anyone make a claim over my mate.

"Is this Aaric the Alpha of his pack?" Kaija asked.

"If he told me the truth when I met him, then he's actually the Beta, though he's certainly arrogant enough to be a pack Alpha. No offense to your father, Princess."

"None taken." She smiled and pulled one leg underneath her. "When you met Aaric, was there anything to hint at his rank? Any response from your wolf that could help us?"

Chest tight, I dropped my head in my hands. "I was using The Draught when I met him. My wolf was…"

"Asleep," Shadow finished what I couldn't. I paused then nodded, pissed at myself for that decision.

While The Draught wasn't necessarily a bad drug in concept, for wolves like us—natural Alphas, trained fighters, the law enforcers in the shifter community with big fucking targets on our backs—taking it was definitely frowned upon. Like Phoenix had said the night before, it was a bad idea to go into a new town without backup and with my senses dulled. Had the local pack decided to come after me for invading their territory, it could have turned from bad to worse. Or even fatal.

"You stopped that shit, right?" Gates asked, his voice hard. I nodded my response, still not ready to look him in the eye. "Good. We need you at full strength. Calla needs you at full strength."

"I know. I only started taking it after Amber showed me my mate and I assumed I couldn't have her because of the baby. I thought it'd help soften the instincts. Instead, I ended up here and all it did was weaken my defenses and put my mate more at risk."

"How did Amber show you your mate?" Kaija asked.

"She performed some kind of spell on me to open up my sight." I snorted a sarcastic laugh. "It opened it up all right. The sight of Calla haunted me, even though I believed she was married or claimed by another because of the baby. I couldn't have her, but I couldn't get her out of my mind. I thought I was going crazy."

"These witches seem like more trouble than not," Shadow said, though the slight curve of his lips indicated a joke.

"That's right," Kaija said with a smile of her own. "You haven't met them yet. Just wait until we get home; you'll like them. They're fun to be around."

"Yeah," I snorted. "Real fun."

"Speaking of home," Shadow said, ignoring my comment. "What about just taking her? Leaving town tonight with Calla and heading east."

I shook my head. "Aaric destroyed her trust in men and shifters. I've been working to prove to her what a mate is and how a mate should treat her, but I don't think we're quite there yet."

"What's our drop-dead time frame?" he asked, looking up my way. I paused, my stomach tight with what felt a lot like fear.

"Twenty-four hours," Gates replied, jumping in and giving me a hard look. "If she isn't ready to come willingly, we're taking her tomorrow night."


WHEN THE STRESS OF being away from Calla got to be too much, we put a hold on our discussions so I could head over to the diner. Gates followed me to my truck, stoic and quiet, as he tended to be when he was thinking. But the quiet didn't last long.

"I think Mom would have really liked Calla." Gates turned to look down the road, focusing on the diner sign. "And she would have loved having babies around again."

"Dad would have adored Kaija's spunk. Fate picked a good mate for you."

He grunted his agreement. We fell back into silence in the cold night air. Anxious, I waited for him to say what he needed to. Because as his brother, I knew the Gatekeeper better than anyone. The quieter he became, the harder his brain was working. It was just a matter of time.

Finally, he huffed. "Some shifters are animals, but so are some humans. Calla not trusting you because you're a shifter is a bit shortsighted on her part. That's an angle you can try. We kill for pack, for family, and for brotherhood. Humans kill for the same reasons plus so many more." He turned to me, his eyes serious. "Have you told her about Mom?"

I blanched, turning away. "No. And I don't plan on it."

Gates growled, his voice dark and serious. "Fate brought the two of you together because you're the best for each other. But you still have to earn that bond. Learn to trust it."

He placed his hand over his ribs where I knew the word "Trust" was inked into his skin. I placed my hand in the same spot on my own, where the words "Above All" had been tattooed on the same day. It was a gesture only the two of us knew, something to remind ourselves that, no matter what, we had each other's backs. That the lies I'd once believed—the untruths that led to our parents' deaths—would never come to pass again. He was my brother, my blood, and we'd each go down in flames for the other.

As his eyes left mine to travel over my face, his expression softened. "You shaved."

"For her."

I stiffened as Gates lifted his hand, spreading his fingers over the claw marks running down my face. The ones nobody had touched until Calla…the same ones Gates gave to me over a century before.

"I haven't seen them since that last night in the desert."

I watched him examining my jaw, knew what was coming before he whispered the words.

"I'm sorry, brother."

I pushed his hand away and shook my head. "No apologies. If you hadn't shifted, I would have killed you."

Gates stood stock-still, staring back at me. Quiet…thinking again.

"This mission," he said, shaking his head. "The way this guy lied and manipulated Calla. It reminds me of that time."

"It's not the same thing," I said, the memories his words dredged up making me want to get in my truck and go. Run. Forget.

Gates' eyes met mine, hard and calculating. "Aaric lied to Calla, twisted our myths and our truths to make her believe what he wanted her to. For his own benefit. How different is it, brother?"

"No one died here."

"Not yet."

I was on him in a second, shoving him into the side of my truck and snarling in his face. "I won't let her die."

"And I wasn't going to let a bunch of humans kill our mother and sister, but I did." He shoved me off him, his eyes glowing with the power of his wolf. "It was my fault the townspeople found out we were shifters. Yet you blame yourself. You've always blamed yourself."

"I should have stopped them."

"They had the cabin ablaze before you came over that ridge. There was nothing you could have done."

A stabbing pain in my heart forced me to take a step back, the memories coming faster and brighter in my head. "I should have been there."

"You and Dad were out hunting for the family, just like Mom asked you to do," Gates said, his voice calm and steady. "Besides, they wouldn't have come if you were home. They would have waited like the cowards they were. They went after Mom because, as pregnant as she was with Aliyana, she was our weakest link. They knew she couldn't fight back the way the rest of us could, so they took the coward's way and went after a pregnant woman. They murdered her and Aliyana, both."

I shook my head and took another step back. "I should have—"

Before I could finish my sentence, Gates slammed me to the ground, kneeling on my chest and leaning down to growl in my face.

"It was me who showed my wolf to a human in town. It was Mom who asked you to go hunting with Dad. It was the humans who came and locked her in the cabin and set it on fire. And it was Dad who gave in to the grief of losing his mate and unborn daughter and walked into that fire. None of it was your fault, and yet you continue to blame yourself."

I lay sprawled on the pavement, barely able to breathe, but

I didn't try to fight him off. Because he was right. In my head, I knew there was nothing I could have done to save my mother and unborn sister. Getting my heart to understand, though, was a lot fucking harder to do.

At a labored gasp from me, Gates leaned back, relieving a bit of the pressure on my chest.

"Is it Calla's fault Aaric lied to her?" he asked, his voice quiet but deadly serious.

I shook my head, still unable to speak.

"Is it Calla's fault she's pregnant with his baby?"

Another shake.

Gates leaned down, practically brushing his nose against mine. "Would it be her fault if Aaric or his men busted into her apartment and stole her away? Kidnapped her? Killed her?"

My growl was deep and violent, but without air to feed it, far quieter than I wanted it to be. My hands gripped his arms, my claws out and ready to defend against whatever threat may come Calla's way. Even if it was my own brother.

"You can see what's happened to her is the fault of a puppet master pulling strings," Gates said. "But not when it's in relation to you. Not when it has to do with the death of our parents."

He stood, lifting his weight from my chest. I gasped and rolled, coughing every inhale, my lungs practically on fire. Gates circled me once, watching, waiting for me to focus back on him.

"You're slowing us down and putting her in danger because she doesn't trust you. But how can she, when you don't even trust yourself?" He walked around the truck, hollering over his shoulder, "Get your shit together and be ready to move her. Trust or no trust, we leave tomorrow night."

# SIXTEEN



LOOKING THROUGH THE FRONT windows of the diner, I sought out Bastian's truck. Again. Like I'd been doing all evening. The man had me tied up in knots inside, more so than I'd ever been before. I'd actually begun to miss him when he wasn't around. That had led to me feeling oddly lonely as the hours passed, which led to staring out the window every chance I got. Not that I got a lot of them.

"Order up!"

Shaking off my doldrums, I rushed to the service window to grab the plates, not needing to check the ticket for where to take them. It was close to closing, and there were only two four-tops with guests. I delivered the food and made sure the family at table six didn't need another refill on their sodas, all without even glancing toward the front door. Victory! But then the bell chimed and I spun, unable to stop myself.

Bastian.

Truly, I didn't even have to look to know he would be the man walking in. I could *feel* him. The loneliness that had wrapped itself around me unfurled, disappearing into the night, replaced by that Bastian-induced sense of comfort I was quickly becoming addicted to. The feeling of home. Of love.

This was so crazy. Everything about the two of us being brought together should have had me running to find help, and yet I stayed, I cared, and I dreamed. Little shoots of faith and hope had begun to grow within me, like the tulips that crept through the snow every spring. Small hints that signaled a new season with new possibilities. Tulips that both thrilled and scared me in equal measure, but still…

Bastian smiled as he looked me over, inspecting me. Top to bottom, his eyes roamed, making sure I was in one piece and unharmed. He did it every time he'd been away, I noticed. As if he feared I'd endured something while out of his sight. It was a sweet gesture, a quiet display of how important I was to him.

"Hi," Bastian said as I walked to him. Steps measured. Struggling for control. I had such an urge to hug him, pull him down to my level and kiss the daylights out of him. Pull his firm body against mine and surround myself with him. Oh, Lord have mercy, I needed him in a way that made me feel crazed and wanton.

He frowned and cocked his head. "How're my girls? You two doing okay?"

"Yeah." My voice sounded whisper-rough, even to my own ears as my heart did a little swoop. The way he included my daughter in his concern was so sweet, it broke down my defenses even further.

Overwhelmed, I shook my head as I looked down, unsure of what to say and not quite comfortable with the truth. I still suffered from doubt—a heavy, heavy burden of doubt—but my heart had decided. After last night and then the talk with Kaija this morning, I knew. I cared for Bastian, more than I'd ever cared for another.

Bastian wouldn't let me hide from him for long. He lifted my chin with a finger, his blue eyes filled with concern.

"Tell me, *cariño*."

I took a deep breath to recenter myself. This was Bastian, my possible soul mate. The man who'd shown up and blown my assumptions about love and shifters out of the water. He deserved my honesty, as I deserved his. So I squared my shoulders and I looked him right in the eye before whispering the scariest tulip of them all.

"I missed you. I'm so glad you're finally here."

His face. Oh, the way it lit up at my words. Big smile, bright eyes, a true aura of happiness radiating from him. I smiled in response, couldn't help it, his joy enveloping me like a blanket.

"I missed you, too," he whispered, inching closer. "And I really wish we were alone so I could show you how much."

"Me too." We stared into each other's eyes for another beat or two, both of us grinning like fools. Being an *us* for a moment.

But reality came crashing in as Mannie yelled my name from the kitchen.

I took a step back, my smile falling. "I have to finish my shift."

"I know," he replied as he slid out of his jacket. "I just thought I'd come early. Maybe grab some dessert before heading to your place."

"You have a sweet tooth, Bastian?" I said over my shoulder as I hurried to the pass-through. Mannie nodded and spun his hand in the air, motioning me to turn the sign to closed. I did as he asked before coming back around behind the counter.

Bastian was watching me, smirking. "Can't a man just like a little pie?"

Heat rushed through me twice. The first time for the dirty thoughts his words brought, and the second for being embarrassed by the way my mind dropped right into the gutter at the innuendo. I was a grown woman, not a twelve-year-old boy. The man should be able to ask for...pie...without me thinking of sex.

His smirk grew, his eyes practically sparkling with mischief.

I narrowed my own.

"You did that on purpose."

"Did what? I was just looking for something a little sweet." His fingers brushed mine on the counter, and the smirk fell to a look of hunger and need. "Something warm and tasty."

My breath caught. Damn that man. I was practically panting for him, and all he'd done was order dessert. Well, mostly.

"Apple, cherry, or peach?" I whispered.

He gave me an appraising look, as if this was somehow a test. "Apple."

"Apple it is." I turned toward the dessert case, but a twinge low in my belly stopped me. Gasping and grabbing the counter for support, I hunched forward as stars exploded behind my eyes. Bastian was on his feet and in front of me faster than I thought possible, crouching to my level.

"What's wrong?"

"Just a pain." I rolled up to my full height, pausing every few inches just in case. Whatever I'd done had hurt, and I didn't want to do anything to cause that pain again. I could still feel a residual pulling on the one side.

Bastian gripped my arm, keeping me steady. "Do we need to call a doctor?"

"No, no, nothing like that. It was just a pinch." I looked into his worried face and gave him the best smile I could. "I'm okay now."

If the look in his eyes was any indication, he didn't believe me. "You should go home."

"I need to finish my shift."

"You okay, Calla?" Mannie appeared behind Bastian, looking over the two of us.

"Yeah," I replied, waving my hand. "I'm fine."

Bastian's frown deepened. "You're not fine."

"Shush."

"Honey," Mannie said, his brows drawn down over his dark

eyes. "If you don't feel well, why don't you head on home? I'll take care of the last tables and clean up."

I shook my head. "You don't—"

"Thanks," Bastian interrupted, gripping my arm tighter. "I'll make sure she gets home."

Outnumbered and too tired to argue, I huffed. "Fine. Let me get my stuff."

"I'll grab it." Bastian guided me to a seat. "You get off your feet for a second."

As he hurried into the back hallway, Mannie smiled. "He's a nice man."

"Yeah, he is."

"When my Norma was pregnant, I was the same way. My overprotectiveness drove her crazy." He patted my hand and turned toward the kitchen before firing a final thought my way. "There's nothing a man won't do for the woman carrying his child. It's instinct."

My heart dropped. *The woman carrying his child.* But I wasn't carrying Bastian's child. I was carrying Aaric's. A man who'd used his claws against me. A man who'd let his friends terrify and assault me. A man who did nothing to help me when it came to his unborn child, a child he seemed to want so desperately.

And then there was Bastian. Always kind, always concerned. Bringing me groceries and talking to my daughter as if she was already here. Caring about both of us, not just one. My eyes stung as tears formed. In a matter of days, Bastian had become more of a father to my child than Aaric could have ever been. And I was so grateful to have him in my life.

I stood as Bastian approached with my coat and purse in his hands, my decision made. When he reached me, I grabbed the front of Bastian's shirt and pulled him down, pressing my lips to his softly, sweetly. He froze for a split second before responding, moving his lips with mine as he leaned into my hold. A few extra pecks for good measure and I released him with a sigh.

He blinked twice, peering down at me. "Not that I'm complaining, but what was that for?"

Hand on his neck, I again pulled him closer, giving him another kiss before whispering, "You are such a good man."

He smiled through his confusion as I let him back up, licking his bottom lip.

"Thank you, I think."

I allowed him to help me with my coat, sliding my arms into the sleeves as he held it. And when he handed me my purse, I grabbed his empty hand and wove our fingers together.

"Take me home, Bastian."

"I thought you'd never ask."

HOURS LATER, AFTER A quick snack and endless conversation with me paying more attention to Bastian's smooth, deep voice than to his words, I lay on the couch as he massaged my feet. There was nothing left to do for the night, no errands or chores to worry about. The apartment was clean, calm, and quiet with no distractions. Nothing left between us...but us.

"C'mere," I whispered, holding my arms out to him. Bastian smiled but capitulated, crawling over me until he covered my body with his own, keeping his weight off of me with his arms.

"Yes?"

I brought my hands to his face, rubbing my fingers over the scruff growing back in. "You're a good man."

"You said that earlier."

"I meant it, both then and now."

Bastian's eyes turned serious. "What's going on, Calla?"

"Nothing, I'm just really beginning to understand how lucky I am to have you here."

He stared down at me, his eyes darkening. His descent to kiss me started slowly, barely discernible. But then his nose touched mine, little more than a nudge. Closer yet, I could feel his breath washing over my face. Eyes closing, his lips finally brushed mine, lightly touching. Soft and reverent. His hand wrapped around mine, joining us, weaving us together, and then he sighed.

"My *cariño*," he whispered before he kissed me strong and deep. I opened my mouth for him, welcoming him, sliding my tongue against his as I moaned and squeezed his hand harder. This man was everything good in life. Safety and warmth, home and care and strength. He was more than I could have dared to hope for.

Feeling sure, settled in my choice, I pushed on his shoulders until he lifted himself off me.

"What's wrong?" he asked, breathless and panting. I smiled and rolled out from under him. Without a word, I held out my hand. He took it immediately, following me as I pulled him off the couch and led him down the hall…to the bedroom. My bedroom.

"Calla." His voice made me pause, made me turn and meet his inquisitive gaze.

"Bastian." I stepped back, still pulling him, leading him through the door.

"Are you sure?"

"No," I answered, smiling through my honesty. "But I'm trying."

He nodded, trailing behind me as I walked to the queen-size bed. There was nothing fancy about my room. Like the rest of the house, it was pretty bare. But this was my private space, my sanctuary, and having Bastian there felt different. More meaningful somehow.

In the dim light of the bedside lamp, I began peeling off my clothes. Giving him a chance to tell me to stop, not that

I thought he would. He stared at me with intensity, soaking me in. When my top and bra were on the floor, he took a step toward me.

"So pretty." His honest words made me smile as I hooked my fingers in my leggings and pulled them down. Baring myself to him.

Bastian's eyes traveled over my body, his hands following. He ran a finger down the side of my breast, over my waist and hip, to the puncture marks wrapping around the front.

"Claws," he growled, his eyes focused not on mine but on the damaged flesh.

"Aaric's packmates."

Bastian's eyes jerked to mine.

"I ran too many times. Aaric got bored punishing me alone."

The growl Bastian let loose was deep and rough, though it didn't scare me. "Did they—" He paused, his lip curling up into a snarl before he shook his head and purposely relaxed his face. "Did they rape you?"

"No. But they..." I shook my head, unable to explain how they'd chased me through the woods. Knocked me down. Terrorized me with threats and claws.

"Calla?"

I took a deep breath and closed my eyes for a second. "I don't like to be pinned down."

His eyes stayed on mine, calm and clear, as he nodded. Still growling, his hand slid lower. His fingers brushing the claw marks on my thighs.

"And these?"

I shrugged, trying to stay calm. "Those are what I get from Aaric when I try to run away."

Bastian's eyes closed, his hand gripping my thigh. "I am so sorry I wasn't here."

"It's okay." I stepped closer, bringing my hands to his chest.

"You're here now."

Bastian nodded, giving me a soft kiss before growling, "They'll never fucking touch you again."

One more kiss, a little hotter than before, and then I stepped back.

"Your turn," I whispered, the soft sound hopefully hiding the shake in my voice.

Bastian didn't hesitate, yanking his shirt over his head from the back of the neck in that way only men can do. Hands on his waistband, pulling open the button-fly of his jeans, he stared at me, eyes bright and pupils wide in the darkness. And then he dropped his pants and stepped out of the denim, deliciously naked before me.

Color. The man was inked from his wrists to his neck and back down almost to his waist. Colors, swirls, words in numerous languages. A walking, talking, breathing work of art. With scars like mine.

I ran a finger down the side of his face and over the lines along his neck. "Claws."

He smirked, probably at the mimicking of his discovery of my own marks. "My brother."

"Lorenzo?"

He nodded. "The townspeople killed my mother when she was eight months pregnant with my baby sister. Burned them alive."

"Oh, Bastian." I gripped his arm and ran my finger over his cheek, encouraging him. He stood before me, brave and bare, his eyes shiny and growing red as he told me his truths.

Bastian pulled my hand to his lips, kissing my palm. "My parents had been mates for centuries, and they truly loved one another. My father was so grief-stricken knowing she died, he walked into the fire to join her, leaving me to figure out what had happened."

"And your brother?" I asked as he grew quiet, his eyes

unfocused, probably lost in his memories.

Bastian's head snapped up, "I thought Lorenzo led the bastards to us, so I fought him."

"Did you win?"

"No one wins against the Gatekeeper."

I moved my fingers to the burns that sat high on his neck, looking into his eyes in question.

"Tit for tat," he growled.

I nodded. His truth should have scared me, or at least made me question being with him. But it didn't. If someone had come after my grandmother, had killed her in such a violent way, I'd want revenge too. I'd want to make the murderers suffer. Nothing Bastian had told me changed my opinion of him or his brother.

"You're so strong," I murmured, rising up on the balls of my feet to press my lips to the bottom edge of his scars.

Bastian sighed. "You're stronger."

"C'mere," I whispered for the second time that evening. Needing more of him. My hands shook as I moved to the bed, sinking onto the mattress, not breaking eye contact.

"You're awfully demanding tonight." He moved toward me, caging me in with his arms as I fell back. "What are we doing, *cariño?*"

"I don't know," I answered honestly. I gripped his arms, needing to hold on to him to keep myself from flying away on a cloud of uncertainty. Needing his strength to be my anchor.

Bastian nodded, angling himself to rest more of his body against mine without putting any weight on my belly. "What do you want?"

I moaned as his body brushed against mine, loving the warmth he gave off, the roughness of his hair on my smooth skin. And I said the only word I possibly could.

"You."

"You're not ready, Calla." He leaned down, kissing me,

teasing my lips with his tongue.

"I think I am."

"If you have to think about it, you're not." He pulled back, enough to look me in the eye. "That's okay, though. I can wait for you." His teeth moved to my jaw, and then down my neck. "I don't want to be inside you until you're sure. Until you're ready for me. All of me."

I angled my head back, closing my eyes. "Bastian."

He slid down the length of my body, spending long, languid minutes lapping at my breasts. Biting my pebbled nipples as I curled my fingers in his hair. Making me moan and writhe from his tongue and teeth. And then he moved lower, rubbing and kissing my swollen stomach. Showing love to me and my child inside. Lower still. Wedging himself between my thighs. He brought his hands to the apex of my legs, spreading me, making me gasp.

"So fucking pretty." He ran his fingers over my flesh, teasing, not touching where I most wanted him to. And I did want him to, with every fiber of my being I wanted him to, right then… that second. But he took his time. Ran his fingers from my knee to my hip, dragged his nose down from my belly button. His hands grasping, rubbing, claiming as they explored.

I didn't notice his head dropping farther or the feel of his breath on my skin, but suddenly his tongue licked over my clit. A spark of pleasure and pressure setting off a bomb inside of me. My body bowed as I squeaked, reaching for his hair again. Fingers threaded through his dark locks, I held on as he licked again. And again. Sucking gently. Running his teeth over me. Driving me mad.

His hands left my thigh, one sliding between my legs, circling where I most wanted him to be. I rocked and moaned, needing. Needing more, needing him, needing something. Something only Bastian could give me. Without my saying a word, Bastian knew what I wanted. He slid two fingers inside, curling them, moving them in and out, adding to the sensation of his tongue and lips as they focused higher.

Shaking, moaning, I held on to his hair as he worshiped my sex, doing my best not to yank his face deeper into me. Not that I thought he'd mind. The sexy growls and groans he made told me more than words could how much he was enjoying himself. How turned on the act of giving me this was making him. But I still wanted more.

For him as well as me.

I pushed his forehead away, leaning up on my elbows to meet his surprised eyes. His lips were swollen and shiny, making me wish for just a moment that I'd let him continue. But I wanted something as well. Wanted to feel him, rub him.

Taste him.

"Swing up here," I murmured.

He didn't move, his eyes wide.

"C'mon." I reached for his shoulders, pulling. "Swing up here. It's not always just about me."

He wiped a hand across his mouth, tongue darting out to taste his bottom lip. I shivered, my entire body on the edge of release as he crawled up and bit my hip.

"I like when it's about you," he said into my skin.

"Bastian, please," I begged. "Get up here before you force me to roll around like a beached whale."

He scooched up my body, placing a small kiss on my breast and licking my nipple before pressing his lips to mine.

"You are not a beached whale."

I rolled my eyes. "I'm offering to suck your dick, and you're focusing on that?"

He laughed long and loud, his forehead on my shoulder. I chuckled with him, holding him close.

"Okay, *cariño*. You win." He spun, lining himself up to my body. "On your side, beautiful."

I rolled, lifting my top leg enough for him to get comfortable.

He laid his head on my thigh, hidden from my sight by my belly. His body almost curving around the front of mine.

"Feel better?" he asked, gripping my thighs.

I wiggled down, supporting my head on my arm, his dick directly before me. Long and thick, it stood straight against his chiseled abs. I reached forward, grabbing him, circling my fingers around him. Stroking from bottom to tip and back, up and down, up and—

"You're pierced *here?*" I asked, my finger running along the steel just under the head.

"Yes," he hissed, his hips rocking as I pulled on the surprising piece of jewelry. I hummed and continued to explore, pulling, sliding, teasing the metal rod. Tugging on the balled ends. Twisting it.

"Fuck, baby," he gasped, thrusting his hips toward me.

"You gave your dick a bow tie." I grinned when he huffed a laugh.

"That's one way to look at it."

I leaned forward, touching my tongue to steel, licking once before grabbing a balled end with my lips and tugging gently. Bastian groaned, his hips flexing.

"I like this," I said, licking it once more.

"Well, thank fuck for that."

I licked the head and ridge before wrapping my lips around him, feeding him deeper, twisting my tongue so I could feel the metal slide along the length. Bastian cursed and shook, his hips thrusting shallowly. Holding back.

I hummed, pulled him from my mouth and lapped at the head, knowing I was teasing him. "You like this?"

He gasped a "Yes."

"Good." I gripped him tight and brought my lips back to the head. "Now get to work."

He let loose a single laugh before I slid him back into my mouth, this time working him deeper, swallowing him down.

He made a sound like a growl and plunged his fingers into me, matching my rhythm. I sucked and stroked as he thrust and lapped. Over and over. Bringing me up to the plateau, pushing me until I couldn't take anymore. Then backing off. Holding my thighs in his rough hands, rubbing my skin until he started the cycle again. Building me up, but not letting me fall. Until he forced me over that edge.

His lips wrapped around my clit, sucking hard as his tongue pressed against me. I came with a swiftness I'd never experienced before, clenching around his fingers as my legs shook. I held on to his dick, rubbing him through my orgasm, bringing my lips back to the head as it ebbed. As I sucked him back in, I shifted my hips away from Bastian's mouth, too sensitive for more. Taking the hint, Bastian moved his lips to my thigh, still kissing and biting, the scruff on his chin adding a warm burn to the action.

I licked and sucked him, increasing my speed on every pass, no longer teasing. Giving him everything I had to give, wanting him to feel as I did. Happy, sated, joined together through these intimate acts. He came within moments, growling through his orgasm, his entire body clenching. I swallowed and kept my hand moving, sliding along his dick, drawing him through the pleasure.

"Fuck, Calla." His back arched, one final muscle spasm rocking his body against mine.

When he was done, when he twisted and spun to reverse his position once more, he pulled me against him. Breathing me in, he tucked his face in my neck. Scenting me. Cradling me to him as I pressed my forehead against his chest and closed my eyes.

# SEVENTEEN

*Beast*

SLEEP HAD NEVER SEEMED like such a waste of time. I had my mate in my arms while her unborn child kicked against my hand. The night pressed in on us, softening the sounds of the highway until they became a whisper in the dark. The waning moon hung low, barely a sliver in the sky, giving the room just enough light to see the edges of Calla's furniture peeking through the darkness. It was the middle of the night, and yet I was awake, alive, completely rejuvenated, and ready.

*I had my mate in my arms.*

Calla's body lay heavy against mine, her back to my front as she breathed deep and even. Though I'd never call our position spooning. I was too wrapped around her for that image, leaning too far over her. I wasn't a spoon; I was a cage made of flesh and fur and instinct. Protecting her and keeping her warm.

Calla huffed as the baby made a big turn, the two of them more in sync than she would ever know. That huff led to her pressing deeper into me, snuggling closer. Which led to her ass wiggling into my cock. Soft against hard, making me bite back a groan as the new pressure sent tingles up my abdomen.

I pulled her tighter into my embrace and buried my nose in

her hair. She smelled of me, which made my wolf side proud. I ran my nose along her neck to her jaw, and then followed that with my teeth. Calla pushed against me again, though this time I couldn't fight the groan as my hard cock got a massage from her ass. I'd been hard all night, but I was quickly moving past aroused. Just the memory of her lips around me, the picture of her with her head on my thigh as she took me in her mouth, was enough to make me want to head to the bathroom to give myself a little manual release.

As she sighed, Calla grabbed my wrist, pulling me tighter around her. I ran a hand down her arm, loving the feel of her soft under my rough. She sighed again, not opening her eyes but pulling my arm tighter around her. Weaving her fingers with mine as I kissed her neck. Bringing our joined hands to her breast as I bit her ear.

"Bastian."

I growled, a deep, dark sound that came from the very pits of my soul. One word, that little whisper, and I was hers. All of me. She could have told me to dress in a fluffy pink bunny suit, and I would have, just to make her smile. God, I hoped what she wanted right then was something better than me in a fluffy pink bunny suit, though. I hoped it was something more adult and carnal.

Calla pressed her hips into the cradle of my pelvis, purposely rubbing herself on my cock. There was no way she couldn't feel me, didn't know how hard I was for her. That move was direct, intentional, and nearly made my eyes roll back in my head.

"*Cariño*," I groaned when she did it again. Calla lifted her arm, bringing her hand to the back of my head and fisting her fingers in my hair, pulling me closer. I tweaked her nipple before sliding my hand around the swell of her breast.

"Mmmm, Bastian." She gasped as I moved my fingers back to her breasts, carefully massaging the sides and tickling her nipples.

"Feel good?"

"God, yes." Her body stiffened in my arms, her legs sliding along one another. She was so worked up already, revved and ready to race, but I still couldn't take the lead. She needed to tell me what she wanted me to do, what she was ready for mentally as well as physically.

I licked up the side of her throat, rolling my hips against hers. "What do you need, Calla?"

"You," she whispered. "Just you."

I worked my hand down from her breast, over her stomach. She spread her legs as my hand slipped between them, my fingers immediately finding her swollen and wet for me.

I growled, loving the feel of her so aroused. "Were you dreaming, *cariño?*"

"Yes." She gasped as I made slow circles over her clit.

"Good dreams?"

"Very good." She pressed on my hand, directing my fingers to move faster, press harder. Her taking what she wanted was such a fucking turn-on, I could have come right then. I growled and followed her instructions. Pressing down, moving my fingers closer to her opening, savoring every sigh and gasp and shiver as she taught me exactly how to touch her. Exactly what she liked.

When she pushed my fingers inside, Calla groaned and let one knee fall to the side, opening herself wider, removing her hand, and leaving mine behind to do the work.

I growled softly and brought my teeth back to her ear, nibbling on her as I whispered, "What do you dream about me, *cariño?*"

Calla moaned, lifting her chin as her hand gripped my hair harder. "I've been dreaming of you taking me in my bed since the night you walked in the diner."

"Jesus, Calla." I plunged my fingers deeper into her wet heat, keeping the heel of my hand pressed against her clit. She responded with a moan and a pull to my hair, riding my fingers as she circled her hips.

"More."

Her whispered plea made me growl louder and pull her back against me tighter. I slid a third finger into her, plunging deeper, thrusting faster.

"Like this?"

"More," she breathed, goose bumps rising along her flesh as her heated skin met the cool night air. She brought her hand back to mine and pushed my fingers inside her harder than I would have been willing to do alone.

"I don't want to hurt you," I said. Instead of answering me, she released my hand, reaching between us to grip my cock. I moaned as my teeth bit down on her shoulder, restraining myself from giving her a claiming bite, but not by much.

"Please," she whispered, her hand sliding up and down on my cock as best she could from such an awkward angle. "Please, Bastian."

"Are you sure you're ready, *cariño*? I can make you come a hundred different ways without going that far." I thrust into her hand, unable to stop myself. She felt so good, and I was so hard. "I could bury my face in that pretty pussy again and lick you for hours if you'd like. Make you beg for release with nothing but the tip of my tongue."

"Oh God." She shook her head and squeezed my cock, making herself clear. "I want you inside me, Bastian. Please."

Feeling like a virgin pup and yet realizing the limitations her pregnant body presented, I buried my burning face in the back of her neck and whispered, "How do you want me?"

She lifted her leg, resting it on top of mine, and pulled my hips against her ass. "Like this."

I shuffled down, gripping my cock and lining myself up with her. "This?"

"Yes." She angled her hips, gripping the sheets as I teased

her with the head of my cock.

"Tell me if it's too much." I slid inside slowly, nudging my way into her heat with whispered curses and deep breaths. So hot and soft. So fucking perfect for me. Calla dug her nails into my arm, fisted the sheets, groaned and arched as I stretched her. The position didn't allow me much in the way of going deep, but that was fine with me. My mate, while strong, was in a delicate state. I didn't want to hurt her in any way.

Tightening my hold around her chest and using my other arm to grip her hip, I began a slow in and out. Long strokes, angling my hips. I kept my head buried in her hair, whispering soft words. Scenting her. Fighting off the need to claim her with my teeth.

"Bastian." She arched more, humming as I increased my pace. "I can feel it."

I growled into her neck. "I sure as fuck hope so."

"No, not you. It. Your bow tie."

I chuckled, thrusting deep before holding still, enjoying the feel of her body wrapped around mine. "Baby, it's a frenum."

"Whatever you call it, it looks like a bow tie." She pushed back against me, making me resume my thrusts. "And it feels so good,"

"Yeah, it does." And it did. It felt so fucking good as her walls squeezed me and pulled me deeper. I slid my hand over her belly and between her legs, spreading my fingers around her clit, matching the strokes of my cock inside her. She groaned as she spread her legs wider, moving her hips in time with mine.

Surrounded by me—one hand on her breast, the other working her clit—my mate was completely at my mercy. And she seemed to like being trapped as she was. Legs stiffening and shaking, hips rolling, she moved in time with my thrusts, her nails clawing at my arm as she approached that point. That cliff between desire and demand. That edge of pleasure-pain right before her orgasm would rush through her. I loved her this way, all breathy and moving on instinct alone, too close to losing control to do anything more than let her body act for her.

"Bastian," she gasped, her every response telling me she was right there, on that cliff, desperate to go over the edge.

"Go, baby. I've got you."

She arched and stretched, her leg falling as her instincts took over. Chasing the high that came from pleasure. And when she came, when her moan turned long and high-pitched, I followed. Clinging to her. Coming inside of her with a growl that shook the bed.

I had to fight back the urge to bite her, to claim her officially. This was my mate. Mine. And she was in danger. I had the means to help her, but the decision was up to her. And I was suddenly banking on the fact that she'd let me into her bed, which had to mean she trusted me. At least on some level.

"Come with me," I whispered as I pulled out. She smiled sleepily and half-turned.

"Pretty sure we both just did that."

I brushed a lock of hair off her forehead, rising onto my elbow to look down at her.

"To Michigan. Leave this place and Aaric and just…come with me to Michigan." I sighed, dropping my forehead to hers and putting everything I had into the words I needed to say. "Please let me make you safe. Come be with me."

She stared for long seconds, her eyes wide and slightly uncertain. Until finally, she said the bravest thing I'd ever heard.

"Okay."

# EIGHTEEN

*Calla*

THE NEXT MORNING, WE pulled up at the diner for my last errand before we headed east. Bastian had wanted to get on the road the second I said okay, but I couldn't disappear without saying goodbye to Mannie.

"So you'll pick me up within the hour, right?" I asked for about the fifth time. The idea of leaving with him, running away, was one I was both scared and excited about. The stronger emotion totally depended on the moment. This being a more scared moment.

Bastian, probably sensing my sudden unease, grabbed my hand. "Yes, I'm just going to run down to the grocery store, and then I'll be back."

"Okay." I played with his fingers, my mind spinning at all the changes coming my way.

"Calla, relax," Bastian said, stilling my hands. "Everything's okay. You're all packed, and Shadow will be at the gas station to watch over you while I make sure you and that little angel have what you need for the drive. I wouldn't leave you alone at all if you'd just let me send Shadow to the store for you."

I shook my head as Bastian grew quiet, feeling his eyes on

me as I fidgeted.

"I'm sending Shadow instead," he said softly. He brought his hand to my cheek to capture my attention. "You're obviously worried. I can stay inside with you while you say goodbye to Mannie."

"No," I said, shaking my head. "You can't send Shadow to run my errands. It's bad enough you're going for me."

"*Cariño*, we need to get you out of here safe and sound. The more places we're seen, the more likely Aaric will hear about it. We've kept everything pretty well under the radar so far; I'm not fucking that up just as we're about to get on the road. If you and me splitting up to finish off these errands keeps you safer than staying together, the decision over what to do gets made pretty quickly."

"I know. I do." I took a deep breath and dropped my chin. "What if Mannie gets mad at me for leaving without notice?"

Bastian lifted my chin with his finger, tilting his head and giving me the sweetest smile I'd ever seen. "Mannie seems like a nice guy. Tell him it's time for you to start your maternity leave, and that you're not coming back. He'll understand. And if he doesn't, Shadow is right there." He pointed to a low-slung black car with tinted windows sitting at a pump. "He'll be watching for you. Walk out the door, and he'll bring you to me."

"And after we leave, we stay together, right?" I asked, clinging to his wrist. "You'll be with me?"

Bastian pulled me closer and pressed his lips to mine before whispering, "If you'll have me."

The double meaning of Bastian's statement made me pause. Looking deep into those blue eyes I'd come to love so much, I felt it. The awareness of things being right. Of us. Kaija had been right—I just needed to get out of my own way to see it.

Bringing my hands to his face, I held his gaze.

"Yes."

His eyebrow rose for a moment before a smile curved up.

"Yeah?"

I nodded, my grin widening. "Yeah."

He pulled me closer, sliding his arms around my hips until I was practically in his lap. Not caring about the world around us, he pressed his lips to mine in a kiss that stole my breath. Heartfelt, honest, and pure, the man kissed me as if his life depended on it. And maybe it did. Because I knew there was no way I could live without him.

When Bastian finally pulled away, I licked my bottom lip, missing him already. "Let's get this over with."

"That's my girl." He ran his thumb over my knuckles. I gave him one last peck before I slid back across the seat. Bastian was out his door and around to my side before I could even get my legs over the edge.

"Show-off," I said, huffing as I dropped into his arms. Bastian guided me to the concrete, shutting the door behind us as I waddled toward the diner.

"You sure you're okay?" he asked, his eyes tight with what looked like worry.

"I'm fine. Just a little sore from last night."

Bastian stopped, his hand on the door handle. "Did I hurt you?"

"No." I sighed when he didn't move, rolling my eyes at how he obviously didn't believe me. "You didn't hurt me, you big ox, but I haven't used a lot of those muscles in months."

Bastian looked me over once more, his worried expression changing to one of desire. "We should fix that. Get you in the habit of using them more often."

I laughed as he opened the door for me. "Animal."

"Just for you," he whispered just before he pinched my ass. I jumped as he chuckled and moved past me, watching as he stalked around the dining area and peeked down the back hallway.

"What are you doing?" I asked.

"Keeping you safe." Bastian hurried over and wrapped his arms around my back. "It's just you and Mannie here, no scent of Aaric or his pack. Just in case, stay inside unless you need Shadow. He'll be watching for you."

I gave him an exaggerated glare and pursed my lips. "Yes, sir."

Bastian growled as he leaned in to capture my mouth with his. Once, twice he kissed me before pulling away. "You sure you don't want me to stay?"

"No. I'll be fine. Besides, the sooner you leave, the sooner you can come back." I gave him one last peck before stepping out of his embrace and heading for the kitchen, turning to give him my sauciest smile. "I may even have a piece of pie waiting for you."

Bastian growled. "Behave, *cariño*. Or I'll say, fuck Mannie's feelings and take you with me right now."

"Soon." I grinned, blowing him a kiss as he backed out the door with a grin. Crazy man.

Shaking off the happy warmth Bastian always brought out in me, I walked into the kitchen, expecting to see Mannie hard at work. Surprisingly, the room was empty.

"Mannie?"

"Morning, Calla," Mannie hollered from the cold storage room. "Aren't you off today?"

I smiled as Mannie walked into the kitchen, his arms filled with trays of meat.

"Let me help you." I took the top trays and set them on the steel counter in the center of the room, swallowing hard before I murmured, "I kind of need to tell you something."

"Oh, I knew this was coming soon." Mannie set down the rest of the meat, his face showing his disappointment even as he tried to give me a smile. "Time for you to go, huh?"

"How'd you know?" My eyes went wide and my stomach dropped. "You're not mad, are you?"

"Mad?" He laughed and shook his head. "Little girl, you always were too good for this place. But make an old man happy and tell me you're not leaving alone."

"Bastian, the guy with the leather coat," I whispered, unable to hold back my smile. "I'm leaving with Bastian."

"Good for you, Calla. He's a good man, very protective." Mannie grinned, his eyes bright. "You three are going to have a great life together."

Heart heavy, I rushed to him, wrapping my arms around his neck. "Thanks for giving me a job."

"Thanks for taking such good care of this place." He pulled back, his eyes glassy and red-rimmed. "You got a few minutes for an old man, or is your Bastian waiting outside for you?"

I shrugged. "I've got some time."

"Excellent. We can talk over a bowl of ice cream before the lunch crowd comes in. I'll even run to the gas station for some of those cookies you like to mix in it." He grabbed his coat from the back of his desk chair in the corner and headed for the front door.

"Thanks, Mannie." I smiled, watching as he hurried through the cold toward the gas station next door. This was it—my last time at the diner and my last day in this nothing town. Soon enough, I'd be sitting beside Bastian as he drove out of town, ready to start a whole new story. The thought made my lips turn up in an unintentional smile and left me feeling almost giddy with anticipation.

But that feeling crashed the second I heard the bang of the back door closing.

"Mannie?" I stepped slowly across the kitchen and past the counter, my heart racing in my chest. Balling my hands into fists, I peeked into the hallway only to find my nightmare glaring back at me.

"Aaric." My voice felt tight, the sound quiet even to my own ears. "What are you doing here? It's daytime."

"Well, I was going to ask how my mate was doing, but apparently the question shouldn't be how, but who." He stalked closer, sniffing me, making the hair on the back of my neck stand on end. "Really, Calla? The dirty animal from the Feral Breed?"

I stood tall even as my fear burned low in my belly. "He's not an animal."

"Oh really?" he laughed. "You think he's not just as much of a wolf as the rest of us? What'd he tell you to get between your legs, huh? How hard was it to get you to spread? God knows I had to work—"

"At least he didn't have to lie to get me into bed."

The smack was loud, knocking my head into the wall and making stars appear behind my eyelids. I clenched my jaw and brought my hand to my cheek, turning slowly to face an enraged Aaric once more.

"Don't push me, Calla." His voice was hard and cold, but I wasn't about to back down. Bastian had given me a chance at a future for me and my baby, and I was taking it. Whether Aaric liked it or not.

"It's over, Aaric." I backed down the hall, heading for the front door. For Shadow.

"Nothing is over until I say it is." Aaric jumped at me, knocking me into the counter, the weight of his body pushing the edge into my back and making me wince. "What…you think this guy's going to rescue you? Take you away from here and give you some kind of life? Wolves are territorial, Calla. He won't want to raise some bastard kid just to get a piece of ass now and again."

"Yes, he will."

Aaric laughed, the sound harsh. "What makes you think you're so special, girl?"

"I'm his mate," I said, practically spitting each word. For a moment, I thought Bastian had driven up outside the door as the floor vibrated beneath my feet. But then I realized it was Aaric growling, and I knew I'd made a huge mistake. Trying to yank my arm from his hold, I started to scream. Aaric punched me in the side of the jaw, shutting me up, the sudden taste of blood making me gag.

"You stupid bitch." Aaric gripped my arm, yanking me almost off my feet as he dragged me toward the back door. "You think I'm giving up over a year's work because you fell for that love at first sight bullshit? The Omega baby is mine; he can't have her."

Kicking the door open, Aaric pulled me outside into the frigid air. For a moment, I hoped that Shadow or Mannie would come to help me. That one of them would see what was going on and somehow save me from Aaric's rage, giving me a chance to get away. But looking around, I remembered there was no way for Shadow to see the back lot from the gas station, same for Mannie as he walked over. I was on my own with an enraged shifter.

Yanking back, I tried to pull my arm from his grasp, but Aaric only held tighter and pulled harder. When we reached the car, he threw me against the side, my wrist screaming in pain as I braced myself to keep from slamming belly-first.

"Get in," he growled.

"No." My tears fell as I tried to take a step back.

Aaric grabbed me by the neck and forced my head down as I yelped in pain. "You will get in this car or I will cut you open from stem to stern and take what is mine."

I sobbed as my shaky hands scrabbled to find the door handle. Aaric smacked my hands away and opened the door, forcing me to walk practically bent in half. Out of options and in too much pain to do much else, I crawled inside the car and began to pray. *Please don't let anything happen to my baby. Please keep us both safe.*

*Please let Bastian find us in time.*

# NINETEEN

*Beast*

I WATCHED MY MATE through the window as she walked deeper into the restaurant before I pulled out of the parking lot with a wave to a watchful Shadow. Soon, just a few minutes really, and we'd be heading to my home. Which reminded me that I needed to make a call. I grabbed my phone and dialed the number to my townhouse, leaving it on my thigh and enabling the speaker.

"It's already done," Amber answered.

I frowned. "What is?"

"Scarlett and I found a place to rent downriver, closer to where Phoenix and Zuri are moving."

"Phoenix bought a house?"

"Yes, but that's not important," she said, sounding frustrated. "You need to get off the phone. And whatever happens, do not let the shadows fall."

"What shadows?"

"I don't know…but everything goes black if the shadows fall."

"I have no idea—"

The click of her disconnecting the call had me looking

down, checking the screen. Nope, I wasn't wrong. She'd hung up on me.

"Crazy witch."

I shook my head as I drove, wondering what the hell she kept talking about with the shadows. Whatever it was, at least she and Scarlett would be out before I moved Calla in. I wanted my mate comfortable, without any awkwardness from having to share her den with other women. Plus, I no longer trusted the eldest Weaver sister, not after the shit she pulled with me. True, putting me under a spell had helped me find my mate, but I didn't like being manipulated that way. And I sure as fuck didn't want to risk Calla or the baby around her.

Seven minutes and one hell of a slow red light later, I turned into the lot of the only grocery store for miles. I was about to pull into a parking spot when my phone rang, making me jump. But seeing Shadow's name on the screen turned my blood to ice. *Calla.*

"What's wrong?" I growled the second I swiped the screen to connect.

"He's here."

My fingers turned to claws as a near-blinding wave of rage burned through me. "Now?"

"Yup. Just pulled through to the back."

Roaring in my anger, I punched the dash, the radio taking the brunt of the force. "Get her, Shadow."

"I'm already on it, boss."

I slammed my foot on the gas, squealing and swerving in a spin toward the highway. "Are you inside yet?"

"No, I'm just about...fuck."

"Shadow?"

"You're Mannie, right?" I heard Shadow say, his voice muffled and distant, as if he wasn't speaking into the phone.

"Goddammit," I hissed, slamming on the brakes as the few cars on the road stopped for the only traffic light in this damn town. Two heavy trucks lumbered through the intersection, blocking my way around. I tapped my claws against the wheel, my leg shaking as Shadow obviously tried to get Mannie to head back to the gas station. Smart, but the old man wasn't my priority. "Get rid of him, Shadow."

Their conversation went on long enough for one of the trucks to clear the intersection, giving me a shot through if I ran the light. Before I could move, my heart nearly stopped for the second time in my life as Shadow barked a "Fuck."

"What's happening?"

I heard an engine rev and a door thump closed just before Shadow came back on the line. "Aaric just peeled out of the lot. He's got her in the backseat."

"Which way?"

"Heading north from the diner. I'm following."

Cursing, I wrenched the wheel to the left and stepped on the gas, whipping past the stopped cars and blowing through the intersection. "Where's Gates?"

"Sending him a message now."

I pressed the gas pedal harder and raced back toward the diner. "Don't slow down to text."

"No worries, man. I'm a talented motherfucker," Shadow said, completely deadpan.

I grunted, my head too caught up in the fact that Calla and the baby were in danger to do much more. "Stay on my mate."

"Doing my best."

The truck's engine roared as I hit ninety-five, flying past what little of the town there was in a matter of seconds. It didn't take long to see Shadow's car far up ahead on the flat stretch of pavement, following a car that had to be Aaric's sedan.

"Coming up behind you."

"I see that." Shadow cursed as Aaric swerved off the road. "He's on a service road."

"Where's he going?"

"Fuck if I know."

I slowed as the turn approached, my heart racing in my chest. I'd promised Calla these assholes would never touch her again, promised I'd keep her safe; I couldn't fail her just hours later.

"Motherfucker." Shadow's curse had me searching the tree line, desperately trying to see past the trunks.

"What's happening?"

"He's got company. Get your ass here."

"Ten seconds." I turned onto the rough road, holding tight to the wheel as my truck skidded across the frozen ground. When the tires regained their traction, I stomped on the gas and flew the rest of the way along the rutted path. The road led to a small snow-covered clearing with two cars idling at the side. One Shadow's, one Aaric's. My eyes immediately searched for Calla, finding her huddled in the backseat of Aaric's car, watching as Shadow and a wolf I assumed was Aaric battled with claws and teeth. My first instinct was to run to her, to get her out of the way, but Amber's words slammed into my memories.

*Do not let the shadows fall.*

Shadows…or Shadow? Cursing the nosy witch and fighting back my instincts, I threw open the door as soon as the truck stopped and shifted in midair. I landed with a roar, paws tearing up the snow-covered ground as I raced toward my denmate, praying it was the right decision.

Two wolves ran into the fray from the other side of the clearing, both of them unknown to me. I slammed into the side of the first one, turning fast to keep the second from attacking Shadow. Battling two shifters wasn't new to me, but doing it while trying to keep track of my mate's heartbeat was. Still, my training served me well. Within minutes of my arrival, the first wolf fell into a pool of his own blood, a victim of my claws. I backed toward Aaric's car, keeping my eyes on the second wolf. He stalked around Shadow and his opponent, who were still wrestling and fighting in the center. I figured we had this, but then all hell broke loose. Five wolves came from out of nowhere, racing across the clearing at the battling pair.

*Do not let the shadows fall.*

My instincts demanded I stay between the wolf in front of me and Calla, that I protect my mate. But Amber…she saw things. She knew.

*Do not let the shadows fall.*

Crouching and snarling, I led my wolf in a half circle, waiting for an opportunity. The squeal of one of his packmates gave me my shot as he turned to check out the noise. I rushed forward, paws slipping a bit on the icy snow, blasting through the wolf and heading right into the fight. Seven wolves on one was almost impossible to win, even seven on two might not end in our favor. But I couldn't leave Shadow alone, couldn't let my denmate fall.

I jumped into the dog pile, snapping and clawing my way through wolves until I found Shadow. Even battered and bloodied as he was, he held his own. Still focused on taking down the one I assumed was Aaric. As much as I wanted the victory of tasting that fucker's blood, I couldn't dive into his fight without risking both our lives. So instead, I backed Shadow up, fighting off the other wolves as much as I could. Wishing for some kind of divine intervention to get me, Shadow, Calla, and the baby out of this mess safely.

I was in the middle of clawing at the eyes of a short, gray wolf when two barks sounded nearby. A pair of wolves raced through the trees toward us, both of them snarling and ready for a fight. One pure white, one solid black. Gates and Kaija had impeccable timing.

The wolf in front of me stumbled as he took in the newcomers, a break I knew I had to take advantage of. I jumped, landing on top of him and clawing through his flesh as my teeth sought his neck. Over and over, I struck and retreated. Taking my own hits and bites, staying on my feet as others fell. But not Shadow. He battled just as hard as I did, his claws vicious, his barks and snarls booming through the crisp air.

Slowly, one by one, we took Aaric's wolves down. Four Feral Breed wolves against seven aggressors. Our skill and teamwork making us nearly impossible to beat. Even Kaija, our newest member, fought like a champion. Keeping the back line secure so none of the pack wolves could sneak by and get to my mate. For that, I would be eternally grateful.

And when the final wolf fell, when his dead body smacked onto the icy ground, I shifted back to my human form and turned toward my mate. Calla stared at me from the backseat of the car, her eyes wide and her heart racing. I knew what I had to look like—naked, claw and bite marks decorating my flesh, covered in blood that was not all my own. An animal wearing a human disguise. Still, I had to get to her. Had to know she was safe.

I stumbled across the ground, ignoring the burn of the cold on my bare feet and the icy wind whipping past my skin.

"Did we get Aaric?" Gates' words registered but didn't stop me. My only thought, my only need, was to get to my mate.

"No. He ran off as soon as Beast pulled up. The one that kept attacking me came out of nowhere, as if Aaric set this up." Shadow said. "If we hurry, we can track Aaric and take him out."

*Don't let the shadows fall.*

"No," I grunted, focused on Calla.

"Beast?" Kaija yelled, her voice concerned.

"We can handle them, Gates," Shadow said.

"No." I stopped, chest heaving, still staring at Calla even as I addressed the rest of the team. "We stay together. We stay with Calla, Shadow."

"But we should—"

"No," I growled, looking his way, my wolf oddly proud as his eyes widened in a moment of what looked like fear. "We stay together. They picked a pregnant human female as their prey, my mate, which cost their pack a lot. They fucked up. Hard." I refocused on Calla, trudging forward again. "I won't do the same. As badly as I want him dead, the shadows will not fall today."

Reaching the car, I grabbed the handle and swung open the rear door. Calla's face was pale, her chest heaving as she practically hyperventilated. But her heartbeat was strong, as was the baby's. I'd done it. I'd kept them safe…I'd fulfilled my promise to her. At least for the moment.

But the biggest test of all was still to come as I held out a hand, praying for Calla to trust me enough to take it. To trust me, both animal and human. To accept me as her mate.

# TWENTY

*Calla*

I JUMPED. THE SECOND Bastian opened the door, standing naked and blood-covered in front of me, I jumped at him. Clinging to him. Crying from the relief of seeing him in one piece.

"Are you okay? Oh my God, I can't believe that happened. Are you okay?"

He clutched me to him, his face in my neck, his arms like steel around me. "I'm fine. How about you? How are my two girls?"

I smiled through my tears as he pulled back to place a hand on my belly, his eyes roaming over as much of me as they could. Completing his inspection.

"We're good," I said. "I think I sprained my wrist, but otherwise we're good." My eyes wandered over him, doing an inspection of my own. Claw and teeth marks decorated his skin, but he was standing and breathing. Which was more than I could say for most of the animals who'd fought in the clearing.

Without warning, the muscles in my abdomen seized, causing me to grab my stomach and gasp from the pain.

"Shadow!" Bastian's roar shattered the quiet of the cold

field, making me whimper. He pulled me closer as I fought to catch my breath, the odd pain fading almost as quickly as it had appeared.

The man from the apartment building, the one I hadn't really met, approached cautiously, long, dark hair blowing around his face. He wore nothing but a pair of jeans and a leather coat, which was way more than Bastian had on.

"You need clothes," I whispered, rubbing my hands up and down Bastian's biceps. I frowned when he winced, apparently hitting a tender spot. "Sorry."

"Not your fault," he said. "Shadow's going to look you over, all right? I need to know you and the baby are okay."

"I'm fine." I pressed my hand to his cheek, keeping his eyes on mine. "Really, I'm fine. That was just a cramp, and the wrist is probably just sprained. A few days with it wrapped and I'll be good as new."

Bastian carefully grabbed my swollen wrist, bringing it to his lips for a gentle kiss. "I hate that he hurt you."

I fingered a long line of scratches on his arm, ending in puncture marks where one of the wolves had gotten ahold of his wrist. "Ditto."

He huffed but was interrupted as the other man moved closer.

"What's needed?" Shadow asked, eyes dropped and head tucked low.

"Calla's got bruises on her face," Bastian growled, taking a step to the side. "And she says she hurt her wrist."

The man smiled at me as he reached out to examine my arm, his deep gray eyes wrinkling at the corners. His movements were slow and deliberate, cautious even. Not that I blamed him; Bastian was staring daggers at the poor guy from his place at my shoulder.

When Shadow looked at my wrist, his brow furrowed. "What happened?"

I winced as his fingers probed. "I was trying to get away. Aaric pushed me into the side of the car, so I—"

Shadow and I froze as Bastian growled, so dark and deep it sent birds to flight in the trees around us.

"Hey," I said, demanding his attention. "Calm down. It's over, and Shadow's just trying to help."

Bastian huffed and looked toward the woods. "Aaric got away. It's not over."

A chill went down my spine as Shadow's nimble fingers moved on my wrist once more.

"You put your hand out to stop yourself from hitting the car? So your weight hit like this?" Shadow held up his hands as if in surrender and pushed forward.

"Exactly." I rubbed my uninjured hand over my belly. "And I've got a lot of weight behind me."

Shadow grinned, a charming boyishness shining through. "Yes, but it's like ninety percent baby and water. You'll lose it all once she's born."

"Really?"

"I have no idea, but it sounds good, doesn't it?" He laughed, gray eyes practically twinkling. The shape of them spoke of some kind of Asian ancestry, adding to that cat appearance I'd noticed the first time I saw him. Handsome. He was definitely handsome, though much more clean-cut than my Bastian.

"What's the verdict?" Lorenzo asked as he strode over to us. He and Kaija were dressed in some kind of flowing fabric things—long and woolen, they covered them from neck to foot.

"Broken wrist." Shadow gave me a grimace. "Sorry, Calla, but you're going to need a cast. I can do it field-style, but I'd prefer if she went to the hospital and got X-rays just in case."

"Fine. I'll take her once we get out of the area." Bastian put his arm around me. "Why don't you three deal with cleanup here?"

"Kaija and I will deal with the bodies," Lorenzo said. "Shadow goes with you."

Bastian frowned. "It'll be faster if it's the three of you."

"You'll be safer if you have backup," Gates replied, eyebrows raised.

Bastian looked as if he wanted to argue, but then he glanced at me. "Yeah, that makes sense."

"Then let's go," Shadow said, wrapping his arms around himself. "I'm freezing to death."

"Grab some clothes from our car," Kaija said, nodding to Beast. "We'll be less than an hour behind you."

"Sounds good," Bastian said. Without warning, he slid his arms around me and lifted me up. "Let's go, mate. I'm freezing my balls off."


"ARE YOU OKAY?"

Bastian's concerned voice roused me, making me realize I'd been shifting in my seat again.

"Yeah, just…uncomfortable." I smiled at his concerned look. "I'm nine months pregnant. Uncomfortable is normal."

"But you moving like that isn't."

I winced as a particularly strong cramp pinched low on the side of my belly. "The doctor said I was fine. I'm just not used to sitting so long, is all."

We'd been driving for hours, well into the night. Bastian had found an urgent care center off the highway just into Minnesota where they'd confirmed a small break in my wrist and applied a cast. To be on the safe side, the doctor had hooked me up to a fetal monitor, making both Bastian and me smile with relief when he said the baby seemed to be just fine.

Moments later, Bastian pulled the truck off the highway.

"What are you doing?" I sat up, looking behind us to make sure Shadow's car was still following.

"There's a hotel at this exit. It's just a Holiday Inn, but it'll do for a night."

"Is it safe to stop?"

Bastian glanced in the rearview mirror. "Shadow's behind us, and my brother was on the road before we left the urgent care center. I'll call him when we get inside so he knows where to meet us." He looked at me, his face hard and almost scary in the shadows. "No one will get near you."

I nodded, too tired to argue. Bastian pulled into the lot of the small hotel, waiting until Shadow pulled up beside us to head inside. I sat in the truck with my head against the window, too tired to hold my eyes open any longer. It'd been a long and crazy day, starting and ending with me in Bastian's arms, with a heck of a lot of drama in the middle. I was relieved it was over, that I was safe with my Bastian and heading toward a new life.

I was almost asleep when Bastian came back, the slam of the door rousing me from my near-nap.

"We can go in through the back." Bastian drove us around the building, parking the truck near the rear entrance. Before I could clamber down, he was there, helping me down and keeping an arm around me for balance.

Shadow unfolded himself from his car, stretching. "Plan?"

"I got you a room." Bastian handed him a few credit-card looking pieces of plastic. "There's a room for Gates and Kaija as well. I told him to get in touch with you when they arrived. I know it's a lot to ask, but I need you three to handle security. I can't..." His voice cracked, and his eyes were soft when he looked down at me. "I can't leave her alone."

"I've got you covered until the cavalry arrives, and then we'll work out a schedule. You two go. I'm sure Calla needs some rest."

As soon as Bastian and I were situated in our room, my nerves crashed and I was left feeling shaky and scared. I tried to push past the feeling, but the harder I tried, the more my heart pounded. The less air the room held. The more—

"Bastian."

My desperate whisper was something instinctual, a call to my mate to help me. And he did. He was behind me in a flash, wrapping one arm around my shoulders and one under my belly. Surrounding me with his heat and his strength.

"I've got you, Calla. It's probably just your blood pressure finally leveling out. It'll pass in a minute."

I nodded, clinging to his arm.

"Breathe with me, *cariño*." His arms tightened, his head resting in the crook of my neck as he bent to press every inch of his body against me. "Just breathe with me. Almost there."

It took several minutes, but eventually, my heart slowed to a normal pace and my breaths matched Bastian's slow, easy rate. He rocked me slightly, humming against my skin, holding me up when I was ready to fall. When I turned in his arms, just enough to meet his eyes, he looked me over with a worried frown.

"You okay now?"

"Yeah," I said with a nod.

Bastian leaned in to kiss the tip of my nose. "And our angel? How's she doing?"

I grinned as I grabbed his hand and moved it higher, to the spot where the baby had been kicking me since Bastian started rocking us. When I pressed our hands to the spot, she gave a mighty nudge, making Bastian chuckle.

"Feels like she's doing just fine in there. Has she moved down?" He turned me a bit more, looking over my stomach. "Your bump looks lower than before."

"Could be. She's supposed to drop at some point before I go into labor." I shrugged and waddled toward the bathroom. "I really want to get the smell of Aaric off me. I'm going to take a shower."

Bastian looked anxious, clenching his fists as he nodded his approval. Tense. He was incredibly tense. That look sparked an idea, which made me grin. I couldn't fight off a pack of wolves by myself or sneak around the halls all hours of the night on guard, but I could help my mate relax.

"Care to join me?" I asked, looking over my shoulder.

Bastian was across the room and picking me up before he even answered, carrying me into the small bathroom as if I weighed nothing. We undressed each other slowly, peeling layers of clothing off and discarding them on the floor. Hands exploring, learning curves and dips as our lips danced softly together.

"I am so blessed," he whispered, his words solemn. I ran my hands through his hair as he knelt before me and helped me out of my pants.

"We're the ones who're blessed."

Bastian looked up at me, moving closer to lean his forehead against my belly. "If he would've hurt either of you…" He kissed my belly, rising to his feet with his eyes on mine. "I'm sorry he was able to get so close to you. That'll never happen again. I don't make the same mistakes twice, *cariño*."

"It's okay," I whispered, reaching to turn on the hot water. "You saved us. You and your friends. That's the important part of today. We're alive and safe because of you."

Once under the spray, Bastian turned me so my back was against his chest again, the only hold where we could press our bodies together. I curved into him, needing to feel all of him. He ran his hands down the side of my belly, taking the weight of it in his hands as he nuzzled my neck.

"You're so beautiful."

I shook my head. "I don't feel beautiful."

"What do you feel?"

"Tired, uncomfortable…a burden." My final word came out on a whisper, something I hadn't truly thought about. But the fact was, Bastian and his friends could take care of themselves. They had strength and abilities I'd never know. I was the weak link in their group.

Bastian growled soft and low as he kissed my neck and rocked me from side to side. "Never. You will never be a burden to me."

"But today with the fight, I couldn't do anything. And now with the move, I'm not going to have a job or a way to pay for things."

"Stop." Bastian turned me, wrapping his body around me from the side. "You're my mate; that means we take care of each other. Whether that's physically or financially, or just putting up with the bullshit I'm sure I'll throw your way. Everything will be fine; the only thing you need to worry about is keeping you and the baby healthy."

"I'll try," I whispered, smiling as his hands roamed. "What's your home like?"

"In Detroit? It's a brick townhouse, three stories tall with a little basement. The building's only a few years old so everything's new. But it's not like your apartment. It doesn't have any of the personality or warmth your home had." He pulled me closer, his lips and tongue teasing my skin. "You can change it however you want. I want you to be comfortable there, to have a real home with me."

I smiled and sighed, loving the feel of his kisses and nibbles, of him growing hard against me. "As long as you don't leave the toilet seat up."

"I've been a bachelor for over two hundred years. I make no promises." He slid one hand up to massage my breast while the other found its way between my legs. Teasing me, running his fingers lightly along either side of me. I sighed when his strokes grew stronger, igniting a fire within. Quickly making me wet and needy for him. When he curved his body over the side of mine, his dick pressing into my hip, I grabbed his arm and stopped him.

"Let's go to bed," I whispered, running my fingertips over the metal bow tie to be sure he understood my meaning. His eyes stayed on mine as he leaned in for a kiss, one sweet peck before he turned off the taps. He followed me out of the shower, gently drying my body with a scratchy towel before backing me toward the bed. His lips met mine again and again, his hands gripping my back and helping me stay balanced. I wrapped my arms around his neck, holding myself up on the balls of my feet as we moved. Needing him too much to allow even an inch of space between us.

When we reached the bed, he turned us around, lying down on the mattress and pulling me on top of him.

"I'm too big," I whispered, wishing there was a way to hide my swollen body from his gaze, no matter how hungry it seemed.

"You're beautiful." He tugged my arm until I smiled and threw one leg over his hips, keeping my weight on my knees as I straddled him.

"I don't feel it."

He pulled me down, raising his head off the pillow to meet my lips. "Give me time, Calla. I'll make you feel beautiful every second of every day."

I smiled into his kiss, groaning as his hands moved up to massage my breasts. They were so sensitive, so heavy and sore at times, but I loved when he handled them. The way his hands could be so strong but so gentle. Rough palms lifting and rubbing my flesh, callused fingers tweaking my nipples, teasing them to hard points. But when he brought his mouth into the mix, when he rose to lick and bite my breast, my body positively shook for him. My gasps and groans coming fast and loud.

Sitting up, gripping his hands for balance, I rocked over him. My soft, wet skin sliding along the hard length of him. Keeping my eyes on his as I teased us both. The way he watched me, the look in his eyes, told me how beautiful he thought I was more than words ever could. Made me feel it instead of just hearing it.

Ready for more than just friction, I reached behind me and wrapped my fingers around his dick to guide him to my opening. He licked his bottom lip as the head slipped inside, his hands dropping to my thighs to hold me steady. Pressing down, I slid him inside of me, my pussy enveloping him as I groaned and tossed my head back. His dick stretching and filling me as he went deep. God, he felt so good. The pressure inside making me crave more. I'd needed this. We'd needed this.

While I gripped Bastian's hands for balance, I rocked over him, setting a slow pace without any sharp movements. Rolling my hips, barely letting him slide out before I brought him all the way inside again. He didn't complain or try to make me move faster. He just lay back, let me do what I wanted. Let me find my pleasure in my own time.

"Bastian," I sighed as the tension grew inside of me. He growled and lifted his hips, pushing up into me on my down strokes. I gasped and shivered, loving the feel of him so far inside, the simple pleasure of being filled by him. When I began to move faster, the want to come quickly becoming a need, he licked his fingers, bringing them to my swollen clit, circling in the way he knew I liked. I rode him and his hand, holding my upper body up with the strength in his arms, rocking hard as I chased my orgasm.

When I came, it wasn't a sudden onslaught of pleasure or a burning need to move faster, go harder. It was a gentle sweeping movement into a wave of sensation. Tingles dancing over my skin from my head to my toes. Inner muscles clamping down on Bastian and making him groan and thrust faster. He followed soon after, clinging to my hips as he growled and shook. Letting himself fall as he held me up.

We snuggled for a long time afterward, both silent, simply

enjoying the feeling of being together. Bastian had me wrapped in his arms again, my back to his front, my body caged within his. He rubbed his hands all over my swollen belly, the baby calm and quiet within.

"I wish I would have met you before," I whispered, still watching his hands.

"Before what?"

I indicated my belly. "Before this."

He was quiet for a moment, though his hands kept moving. And then he turned me, laid me on my back and raised my chin to look me in the eye.

"I don't wish that at all. You're giving me a family right from the start instead of making me wait. I count that as a blessing, not as something I wish could be different. This little angel is a part of you, and I get to raise her as my own with you by my side. I couldn't ask for more." He slid down the bed, resting his face against my bump and raining soft kisses over my skin. "I'll be there for both of you. Teach her what it is to be a wolf, as well as a human. Show her how to be a good one of each. She'll be mine in every way that counts."

I smiled as the tears fell, happy tears filled with emotion for this incredible man. Bastian trailed his lips up my body, murmuring his feelings over and over as he turned me on my side and slid back into me. Holding me close. Showing me with his words and his body how much he felt for me. How much he cared for me. Mirroring all the things I felt for him.

And when we were finished, finally sated and sweaty, I rolled off the bed.

"Where are you going?" he asked, lifting his head from where it laid on his arm.

"Just a quick trip to the bathroom then I'll be back."

Bastian groaned and rolled, curling around my pillow as he watched me. I smiled and shook my head, feeling sexy and wanted as I walked naked across the room. But that feeling didn't last for long. Gasping, I gripped the doorframe as a strong cramp gripped my midsection, nearly doubling over at the pain. Bastian was up and at my side in a breath.

"What is it?"

"I don't know." I closed my eyes, willing the pain to stop.

"Do you think we should get you to a hospital?"

"No," I said, rolling to my full height as the pain ebbed. "Aaric said hospitals would be risky, that she could be born in her wolf form."

Bastian sighed. "It doesn't happen often, but it does happen."

"Then, no. No hospitals for her birth. I can't risk her." I stood straight as the pain receded enough for me to breathe again, smiling at Bastian to prove I was better. "See? I'm fine."

Bastian didn't look convinced, but he let me go into the bathroom alone. I shut the door behind me, breathing a sigh of relief as I rubbed the painful spot on my side.

"C'mon, baby," I whispered. "Just let us get you to your new home before you say hello."

I'd taken three steps across the room when my entire abdomen locked down in the biggest cramp I'd ever experienced. I fell forward, my knees hitting the tile when I missed the sink, crying when my wrist smacked the edge.

"Bastian!"

# TWENTY-ONE

Beast

*Twelve Weeks Later*

"THIS AIN'T MY FIRST rodeo, man."

I growled as Phoenix stood in my doorway, mocking me with my own words. He'd been a right cocky prick ever since I'd showed up in Detroit with an exhausted Calla and a tiny bundle of pink in my arms. Speaking of which...

"I don't think I should let them take you," I whispered. My sweet Aliyana made the gurgling sound I'd come to accept as a yes and grabbed my beard. Little fingers tugging on my chin. I was thankful my facial hair grew as fast as it did. The baby loved my beard almost as much as her mommy did.

"Really, Beast. I babysat a lot as a teenager. I can handle Ali for the night, even with my other child here." Zuri thumbed in the direction of Phoenix, who looked affronted.

"Hey, I'm not a child."

I snuggled Aliyana closer as she hung on to my beard. For the past twelve weeks, Calla or I had been with her every second. No babysitters, no leaving the townhouse without her coming along, and no time alone. And we'd loved every second of it. But all that togetherness meant one thing—no adults-only time. Hell, Calla'd been given the all clear to put her pussy back in business weeks ago, but we'd been so busy with the baby, we hadn't had a chance to do anything. I was pretty sure my balls had turned into blueberries about six weeks back.

"Are you going to give her up?" Zuri asked, looking at me with a smile.

I growled and held my princess closer. "Never."

Poor Calla had gone into labor in that cheap hotel room off the side of the highway. Shadow had come to help when I'd called and so had Kaija. Even with no medical training, my brother's mate had been a tremendous help. She'd assisted her packmates birth pups and babies from the time she was still a young girl, so she knew the ropes. Which was good, because I was pretty fucking useless.

After hours of Calla walking in circles, hanging from my neck, and breathing hard—all while I did nothing but fret and piss her off—Kaija had told me to get behind my mate and hold her up.

"And for the sake of the gods, don't say anything stupid."

I didn't speak a word during the entire three-hour process of Calla pushing.

But when Aliyana had appeared, all slimy and wrinkled and screaming like a banshee, I couldn't stay silent. I whimpered for about a minute before I finally let loose a howl my wolf spirit was awfully proud of. One of celebration and family. Calla had held the baby first of course, letting the tiny thing nuzzle her breast. But after only a few moments, she'd handed me the tiniest bundle of sort-of human flesh I'd ever seen.

It had been love at first sight…for both of us. My angel, my beautiful baby girl, had grabbed my heart—both man and wolf—from her first breath, and she wasn't letting go.

"Bastian."

My mate's voice had me spinning to find her, something

instinctual, like the way I reacted when Aliyana cried.

"Hey, Calla," Zuri said with a wave as Calla rounded the corner into the living room. "We're just trying to tear that gorgeous little bundle away from your mate. No success yet, I'm afraid."

I growled. Aliyana made a sound like a giggle and squirmed in my arms. She loved my growl. She loved it even more when I was in wolf form. That two-month cliff of not sleeping had been brutal with her. But we'd figured out if I shifted to my wolf and let her lay up against me while I growled, she'd sleep through a brass band in the same room. I'd spent a lot of time in my wolf form the past few months.

"Yeah, getting these two apart can be a bit tricky." Calla smiled at me, reaching to cup the baby's head as she whispered, "It's just one night."

I tightened my hold. "What if she needs us?"

"They'll call."

"What if she can't sleep?"

"Phoenix can shift and cuddle with her."

"What if—"

"Bastian." Her sharp tone had me clamping my jaws together. "It's one night. We need this time alone for our relationship, remember?"

I sighed even as my cock grew hard thinking of all the possibilities for the night. "Yeah, yeah, I do."

Our relationship, which meant sex in Calla-speak. That'd been put on hold while we bonded with little Aliyana. Deservedly so. But I'd missed the physical side of being with my mate, and Calla felt the same. So we were taking this night—an official back-in-business night—to ourselves for a little reconnection. I'd been looking forward to it. My cock had been damn near counting the seconds. I mean, it'd been three months since I'd gotten anything more than a pat on the ass as Calla walked past; of course I was looking forward to it.

But now that the time had come to hand over our daughter to someone else, I was panicking.

And she was our daughter. My daughter. No one could tell me otherwise. Let Aaric try to come back and claim her as his. I'd rip him to pieces before he said her sweet name. Besides, I already had plans in the works for that fucker. Plans to keep my girls safe and remove the shadow hanging over our heads. Aaric wouldn't escape the Beast of the Feral Breed again.

"Bastian," Calla whispered, her voice all warm and sexy against my ear. Well, damn, the woman was pulling out all the stops.

Taking a deep breath, I leaned over Aliyana and gave her a kiss goodbye on her forehead. "You be good. Don't give *Tía* Zuri any trouble." I glanced at Phoenix, smirking. "But make sure to spit up on *Tío* Phoenix. He deserves it."

"Hey!" Phoenix exclaimed. His mate giggled.

"Quit crying. And Beast, don't worry. I've got this under control." Zuri moved in to take the baby from me, but we hit a snag in the way of Aliyana herself. Calla had to untangle the baby's fingers from my beard, which caused Aliyana to start crying. I knew how she felt—I didn't want to let go either. Calla cuddled our little angel close, calming her down with pats and rocks, bouncing a bit where she stood.

"Besides," Phoenix said, reclaiming my attention. He hoisted the bag we'd packed for them and threw an arm around Zuri's shoulders. "This'll be good practice for us. For August."

I cocked my head as Calla gasped and Zuri grinned. "August?"

"I'm pregnant," Zuri said, looking so happy and filled with joy she could have lit up a room. Calla rushed to them, hugging and congratulating the pair, her excitement obvious.

I smiled, leaning in to kiss Zuri's cheek. "Congratulations."

She grinned, the picture of excitement. "Thank you."

When I moved to Phoenix, I saw the same concerns in his

eyes that I felt at the news. It was too soon to know what aspects of each parent made up the little one Zuri was carrying in her womb. The baby could be half witch, could be half shifter, or could be none of the above. But being that there was no record of witches and shifters mating, their resulting children could have any number of paranormal powers, which had the potential to make them a target. We'd have to wait and see, but until then, Zuri'd need one hell of a guard force around her.

"Congratulations, my boy." I gripped Phoenix's neck and pulled him into a hug. Keeping my voice down so the women couldn't hear me, I whispered, "We protect our family at all costs."

Phoenix slapped my shoulder, staring into my eyes with a strength that made me proud. "Yes, we do…brother."

I nodded, so damn proud to call him my family. Phoenix had grown into one hell of a strong man; I knew he'd bust his ass to keep Zuri and the baby safe. Wanting to break the heavy feeling I'd created between us, I smirked at him.

"And just wait, fucker. Say goodbye to things like sex and sleep and not smelling like vomit."

He rolled his eyes, still grinning. Calla handed our now-calm baby to a waiting Zuri and tucked the blanket around her. I growled low, the fear of my baby being out of my reach making me and my wolf twitchy.

"I'll miss you, my sweet angel," Calla said, giving the baby a small kiss to the forehead. "We'll see you in the morning."

I moved closer, fighting not to take the baby back and run upstairs. Calla and I needed this break; it was just so hard to take it. Holding Calla's hand, I mentally committed to letting Aliyana go with Phoenix and Zuri. And to have sex with my mate as soon as the door closed behind them.

"Bye, baby. Daddy will be here if you need me." I met Zuri's gaze. "Really, just call us if you need anything."

"We'll be fine," she said as she wrapped the baby up in an

extra blanket. "Say bye to Mommy and Daddy, Ali."

My heart broke as Zuri and Phoenix walked out the door, taking my baby with them. I may have even whimpered when the latch clicked.

"She'll be fine," Calla said, rubbing my arm.

"I know she will, it's just"—I huffed and dragged a hand over my beard—"it's hard to watch her go."

"Yeah, it is." Calla snuggled into my side, running her hand over my chest. Along the ridges of my abs. Down to palm my cock over my jeans.

"Bastian?"

I groaned as she gripped me, my mind going from daddy mode to mate mode in a blink. "Yeah, *cariño*?"

"We're alone."

I rocked my hips, quickly hardening at her touch. Damn, twelve weeks with her soft body pressed against mine in bed but no…anything. I'd practically chafed my poor soldier, having jacked him so much in the shower. He'd never been cleaner. But the war was over. He could finally go back home, to the place he was made to be.

"I'm going to get cleaned up." Calla gave me a final rub.

"I'm just going to get you dirty again." I watched her walk away, a low growl rumbling in my chest at the seductive sway to her hips. "Besides, I'll take you any way I can get you. Clean, dirty, doesn't matter."

She shot me a wink over her shoulder and disappeared up the stairs. I followed slowly behind her, strolling into the nursery out of habit. Pink and bright with white furniture, the room screamed baby girl. The crib sat on the far side, away from the windows in case of a draft. Gates and I had spent an afternoon cursing and hitting each other as we put the damned thing together, but that had all ended when I'd told him the baby's name.

"I want to name her after our sister," I'd said, looking him in the eye. "Pick up where Mom and Dad left off. Maybe take the bad memories and push them behind the good ones."

Gates had smiled. "I think that's a wonderful idea. Mom would have loved it."

I grabbed Aliyana's teddy bear, the one Rebel had brought over the first time he met her. He'd been enamored of her immediately, his eyes straying to his mate Charlotte every few minutes.

"Don't even think about it, Abraham," she'd said, scowling at him. "I am nowhere near ready for that kind of step. That's not even a step. I'm barely a foot off the ground, and you want to climb Mount Everest. Not happening."

I'd grinned at him. "Isn't the guy supposed to be the one afraid of commitment?"

"Not in my world, man."

Missing my mate, I strolled into our bedroom. Calla was still in the en suite doing whatever women do to clean up before sex. Because really, that's what was about to happen. Sex. Lots of hot, dirty, making-up-for-lost-time sex. If she ever came out of the bathroom.

I walked around our room, touching all the little extra things that had been added since Calla moved in. Everything about my life had changed since we'd gotten back. Amber and Scarlett no longer lived with me. I'd moved Yard Shark Customs to Detroit so I could rely on the backup of my Feral breed denmates while keeping my girls safe. On the nightstand where once there was nothing but an alarm clock stood a video monitoring base so we could keep an eye on Aliyana. The top of the dresser that had never had a thing on it was now covered in picture frames, each one filled with pictures of the two women who ruled my world. Pink blanket on the chair, a tiny sock on the arm. Calla and Aliyana had taken over, adding personal items where once there was bareness. And I'd never felt so fucking blessed.

"Bastian?"

I turned, smiling, but my smile quickly fell. Good fucking God, she was trying to kill me. I'd thought she'd get all fancy for our cleared-for-sex night. Maybe a little black lace, some ribbons and heels. All the trappings women used to make themselves feel sexy. Not that I would have minded. But my mate knew me better than that. She stood in the doorway to the bathroom, hair up in a high ponytail, no makeup on her face. Wearing nothing but one of my Feral Breed T-shirts and a smile.

"Are you ready for me?" she asked, raising one eyebrow.

Yeah. Yeah, I was. Totally, completely, entirely ready for a life with this woman.

"Ready?" I snorted a laugh, reaching behind my head to pull my shirt off before unfastening my jeans and pushing them down my legs. I wrapped my hand around my cock as she moved closer. Stripping off the T-shirt, she pressed her naked body against me, her hand joining mine. I directed her fingers to the frenum piercing she'd gotten such a kick out of all those months ago.

"I'm wearing my fucking bow tie and everything, *cariño*. Just for you."

Lips meeting, hands working together to stroke me from base to tip, I was in a full state of bliss. My mate had my heart, my soul, and my body in her very hands. And I couldn't be fucking happier about it.

A shifter of a different breed.

A woman trying to outrun her past.

*A forever even fate can't promise.*

# ACKNOWLEDGMENTS

Once again, I have to say thank you to the readers of the Feral Breed. You continually surprise me with your kind words and support as I spin these tales. Keep the shiny side up, all.

To Maria Clara of the Feral Breed Reader Group, who made sure I didn't embarrass myself by helping me pick the perfect Spanish term of endearment from Beast to his sweetheart.

To Lisa, who never tires of giving me advice or fixing my ridiculous comma errors. We're not quite done yet, lady... Time to gird the loins!

To Caren, who is the only person I could talk about sex toys with before breakfast. Don't ever doubt that I love you or that I miss you when I disappear into my writing cave.

To Esher, who never fails to make me think about what I write and how it can be better. New York bound, baby!

To Anna, who writes sexy shifters and doesn't let me skimp on the drama. I'm really thankful to have found you.

To Angelita, who's new to my circle of writer friends but who definitely helped me with this beast. Get it…beast? I'm so not funny.

To Heather, whose spirit and faith inspired a lot of Calla for me.

# ACKNOWLEDGMENTS

To Brighton, for eating cheesecake with me while we talk about the business, both good and bad. You're still a rockstar, lady!

To my husband, who makes our little girls laugh so hard, you can't help but join in.

To all the folks in the Feral Breed Reader Group, to my Twitter friends, the author groups on Facebook, the writes of the FF&P RWA group, my new friends at the Chicago-North RWA group, and to the authors over at Romance Divas, thank you again for keeping my world so broad. You deserve even more cookies for the entertainment, instruction, and motivation you've provided me with.

Edited by Silently Correcting Your Grammar, LLC
Cover Art by Cormar Covers

# ABOUT THE AUTHOR

A storyteller from the time she could talk, Ellis grew up among family legends of hauntings, psychics, and love spanning decades. Those stories didn't always have the happiest of endings, so they inspired her to write about real life, real love, and the difficulties therein. From farmers to werewolves, store clerks to witches—if there's love to be found, she'll write about it. Ellis lives in the Chicago area with her husband, daughters, and a giant dog who hogs the bed.

Find Ellis online at:
Website: www.ellisleigh.com
Twitter: https://twitter.com/ellis_writes
Facebook: https://www.facebook.com/ellisleighwrites

www.ingramcontent.com/pod-product-compliance
Lightning Source LLC
Chambersburg PA
CBHW020636110726
47899CB00002B/795